THE BEACH OF FALESA

The Beach

BASED ON A STORY BY ROBERT LOUIS STEVENSON

# of Falesá

BY *Dylan Thomas*

A SCARBOROUGH BOOK
STEIN AND DAY / *Publishers* / *New York*

The publishers wish to express their gratitude to Jonathan Fox.

SECOND SCARBOROUGH BOOKS PRINTING 1983

The Beach of Falesá was originally published in hardcover by Stein and Day / *Publi*

Designed by David Miller

Printed in the United States of America

STEIN AND DAY / *Publishers*
Scarborough House
Briarcliff Manor, N.Y. 10510

Library of Congress Cataloging in Publication Data

Thomas, Dylan, 1914–1953.
    The beach of Falesá.

    "A Scarborough book."
    I. Stevenson, Robert Louis, 1850–1894. Beach of
Falesá. II. Title.
PR6039.H52B4 1983   823'.912   83-42963
ISBN 0-8128-6205-8 (pbk.)

THE BEACH OF FALESA

It is the hour before tropical dawn, on the hushed, grey open sea. A boat glides by like a shadow, the moon going down behind her tall sails. The boat sails on, through the very slowly lightening night, through moonlight and music, the soft sea speaking against her sides, and is gone again.

Now, it is nearer dawn, and the moon, still bright, lowering towards the glassy, quivering western rim of the South Sea. To the east, the great sky about-to-dawn is cloudless. And out of darkness, into dying moonlight, into rising dawn, the boat glides again.

A bird circles above it and wheels, crying sad and high, then flies away.

The boat is a fore-and-aft schooner, of about a hundred tons. Two dark figures stand on the little deck, looking out into the neither night nor morning. The tall, broad, bareheaded figure, Wiltshire, his hair tossed in the wind, stands still, upright, tense and quiet. The short figure, the Captain, at the wheel, raises an arm to point.

Captain: "There, over there! D'you see? Behind the break of the reef . . ."

He speaks softly, intimately.

Dawn rises, darkness drains suddenly away from the cloudless sky, and the cries of birds begin to be heard as from far away and coming nearer, the cries of the wild duck and the man-o'-war hawk, the awakening Pacific sea fowl. A solitary bird flies towards the line of the island, the lofty, distant, wooded hills and the stretching shore.

Captain: "D'you see? Falesá. That's Falesá, the last village to the east." The Captain hands a pair of glasses to Wiltshire, who puts them to his eyes.

Through the twin circles of the glasses he sees the surf beating against the high cliffs, the thickly treed valleys, the spurs of mountains, the majestic woodlands, the white flash of streams down the glens, the tumbles of waterfalls, the tall breadfruit trees, the coconut palms, the scattered bamboo houses under the trees, and a few tails of smoke wisping up the sky.

Captain: "D'you see that bit of white there to the eastward? That's your house, Mister."

The circles of the glasses move slowly to pick up a glimpse, between palms and breadfruits, of a white bungalow standing high above the beach.

Captain: "Built of coral. D'you see? Best station in the South Pacific. Strong and pretty and broad in the beam, easy to manage and used to knocking about, just like the women."

Now, as he speaks, the circles of the glasses drop. The island is, suddenly, quite far away again, a mountain line, a reef, a distant scatter of trees, and unidentifiable stretch of surfed beach.

Wiltshire, the glasses dangling in his hand, still stares at the Island, and speaks as though to himself: "I can see the starfish in the water and the parrot fish—red and purple and green."

The Captain shakes his head slowly.

Wiltshire: "Can you smell the wild lime? Trees and flowers, hibiscus and pomegranate." Softly, "I've been down near the line too long—*low* down."

The Captain raises his head to the land wind, sniffs, turns on the deck, and shouts below as loud as a bull with a megaphone and in a voice startlingly unlike the soft, intimate voice he has been using: "Ngavindi! Ngavindi!"

He speaks over his shoulder, again in his soft voice, to Wiltshire: "Breakfast, Mr. Wiltshire."

And a cockerel crows. A Kanaka boy appears and takes the wheel.

Great bunches of oranges decorate the stern of the boat; there are bunches of bananas hung from the topsails and stays. There is a chicken coop on the lower deck and one cockerel inside it. It crows to the tropical morning. As Wiltshire and the Captain pass the coop, the little mild Captain bends for a moment down towards the cockerel, and, very quickly, makes a slitting movement with his fingers across his own throat.

Captain, to the cockerel: "Tomorrow, Mister—"

In the Captain's cabin, Wiltshire and the Captain sit at a small duty table laid with glasses and a bottle of gin.

Captain: "Who's going to be mother?"

Wiltshire half fills the glasses. He is a broad, dark-haired man in the middle thirties, stubbled about his broad jaw, shadowed under the eyes by dissipation or fatigue. He has a reckless twist to his mouth, but his eyes are contemplative, a man accustomed to some brutality and much loneliness, to excess and remorse. He looks into his glass, moving it slowly. A ship's clock ticks on the cabin wall behind him.

The Captain, bald and small and ageless, benignly wrinkled, deeply tanned and sea-blown, an old salt soak, soft-mannered rogue and prop of all the Pacific bars, gossip of the islands, raises his glass: "You've got the best little trading station I ever seen." He drinks. "All shipshape and Bristol, clean as a skipper's cabin—" He darts a sly look around the cabin. "Maybe cleaner—snug as a pub in the snow, trim and homey, three rooms all spit and polish, you could drink off the floor. When Johnny Adams saw it—Johnny Adams with the club foot, him that was here before you—he took and shook me by the hand—this one with the mermaid on it."

He makes the tatooed mermaid on the back of his hand belly-dance as he speaks: " 'I've dropped into a soft thing here, Conrad,' he says. 'So you have,' I says, 'soft as fevvers.' "

The Captain looks at Wiltshire's glass: "Your breakfast's getting cold. I only saw him once after that—coughing and weeping, gibbering when it grew dark, peeping and sneaking and spying through the window chinks when the night comes on, squealing in his sleep like pigs. He couldn't get on with the natives or the whites or something. He carried a gun day and night but he couldn't have shot a whale; his fingers twitched, like this . . ."

He reaches to the bottle, refills the glasses. Wiltshire rises, huge in the little cabin, stares through the portholes at the rapidly nearing island, woods, trees, mountains, beach, the sounding surf, houses, and natives on the beach.

Captain: "Next time we came round, he was gone. Vamoosed. Took a chance passage in a ship from up west. Case saw him off." As he is speaking, a boat leaves the beach and moves toward the schooner.

Captain: "See a boat coming yet?"

Wiltshire nods, without turning.

Captain: "*That'll* be Case. *Mister* Case." The

Captain gets up and goes toward the cabin door, followed by Wiltshire.

On the deck of the schooner, Wiltshire and the Captain walk toward the side nearest the island and the approaching boat.

Captain: "He's a *hard* case, too. But he plays the accordion beautiful. And see him playing cards! He'd strip the tattoo marks off your back! Very educating! Went to a fine school, too, back in England, but he got kicked out of there. Something he'd done. Bigamy, p'raps it was, I've forgotten. Yes, that's his boat. Whistling Jimmie fell out of that boat one night and was drowned when he was drunk! That's a horrible death, drowned when you're drunk. Up comes all your past life in front of you and you're too boozed to see it."

Wiltshire: "Sweet place, Falesá!"

The Captain is mildly indignant: "The climate's very wholesome! Look at old Captain Randall, been drinking here like a herring for thirty years till he almost growed scales."

The boat from the island comes nearer. It is rowed by two Kanaka boys, and a white man sits in the stern.

Captain: "What'll you bet he ain't after buying gin? It's gin and cigars and then it's gin and *no* cigars and then when all the parleying's over he starts again with gin—he's an easy man to trade with, but very monotonous."

He waves to the approaching boat. The man in the stern waves his straw hat back.

Captain: "See his striped pajamas and his little cigaroo? Very smart. Johnny Adams, he thought he was a damned sight *too* smart . . ."

Wiltshire: "Tell me about this—Johnny Adams. What was he frightened of?"

The boat has drawn up to the schooner's side. The cock crows again. Case climbs aboard. He is a smallish man, strong and wiry. His nose is hawk-hooked, his black beard neatly trimmed. His face is deeply lined, but whether by age or by illness or by a tropical disease of the past it is hard to tell. He carries himself with debonair confidence. He is dressed in perfectly laundered striped pajamas. He takes off his panama in a salute, first to the captain and then to Wiltshire. His jet black hair is oiled flat back and glistening on his narrow head. He smiles, and when he speaks, it is in faultless, cultivated English. He speaks not ostentatiously, but almost with wry reluctance, with an amused undertinge of self-contempt for his poise and mannered diction so incongruous in their settings, so incongruous as held and spoken by a small, beaked, bearded man in pajamas on board a dirty trader outside a remote South Sea Island.

Case: "Good morning, Captain. The compliments of Captain Randall and myself. He is distressed he cannot pay you his own compliments in person. A slight indisposition. He has the sensation of something unpleasant floating about willy-nilly between his scuppers and his hold. I tell him it is the original South Sea Bubble."

As he speaks, the Kanakan crew is bringing loads of copra from Case's boat on to the deck of the ship. The Kanakas hurry to and fro with their burdens across the narrow deck each side of Case, but they in no way disturb his measured, urbane eloquence. He turns, smiling to Wiltshire and politely, interrogatively, raises his eyebrows.

Captain: "Mr. Wiltshire, Mr. Case."

Wiltshire holds out his hand. After a barely perceptible pause, Case offers his and they shake.

Case: "A delightful name, Mr. Wiltshire. A delightful county. I myself am a Shropshire Lad. As a rival trader, may I be the first to say: Welcome to Falesá! I can recommend the food but not the liquor. The wild pig is delicious. You will like my partner, Captain Randall, too."

Captain: "How much copra you got this time, Mister?"

Case glances casually at a sheet of paper in his hand: "X tons."

Then, with an ironical smile, he addresses himself to Wiltshire: "Copra, Mr. Wiltshire!" He makes a gesture of wry distaste towards the Kanakas unloading the copra. "To think that both our livelihoods depend upon the indigestible interior of the coconut! We sell tinned salmon, washing blue and treacle to the gullible Islanders so much happier without them, and receive in exchange the dried kernels of coconuts masquerading under the dark, charmed name of copra. Copra! Coconuts! My immortal soul is bound up in coconuts! Odious hairy coconuts! And to think that all I knew about them, long, long ago was that one threw little wooden balls at them and never knocked them down!"

With a sharp gesture he beckons to one of his own Kanakan crew: "Here! King of gluttony!" He speaks to the Kanakan fluently in the native dialect, then turns apologetically to Wiltshire. "I have instructed my boys to take your things to your bungalow. Nobody will interfere with them. Everyone is honest in Falesá, except about chickens, tobacco, penknives and women."

And the Kanakan crew is beginning to unload Wiltshire's trading goods into Case's boat: chests and cases, barrels and bales. Case turns to the captain, hands him his sheet of paper: "And now, Captain!"

The Captain reads the paper: "Gin, Cigars. More gin. Gin again. Gin again. You'll be smoking yourselves to death one fine day, Mr. Case."

The Captain and Case move off. Wiltshire stands alone, gazing at the island, as the native boys hurry all around him about the unloading. Seen much nearer from the sea, the island seems to dip and rise, the giraffe-like coco palms bend down as though to graze.

Case and Wiltshire sit together in the stern of Case's boat. It is loaded with Wiltshire's goods and with cases of gin. The two Kanakan boys are rowing. On the island, Case and Wiltshire see the feathered mountains, and land heaving up in peaks and rising vales, falling in cliffs and buttresses crowned by clouds. Along the beach men and women and children stand waiting for the boat to come in.

The high, gay cries of the children can be heard above explosions of the surf. Case, reclined at ease in the stern, lazily indicates the waiting natives: "The committee of deception! All in its Sunday best! It's a festival day. There hasn't been another trader on this island since your predecessor—Mr. Adams. Look at 'em! Everything that can walk or crawl. Women, children, dogs, lizards, and—girls."

Case turns his head slightly in Wiltshire's direction and says casually: "We must get you a wife."

Wiltshire: "Yes, let it wait. I'll have a look around. I'm used to being alone. What frightened Johnny Adams off the Island?"

Case: "Mice. He drank so much native spirit the mice ran over his bedclothes like bison. He used to hear noises up in the bush, terrible strange noises. It was his mice, with bugles. He used to see devils, so they say. Take no notice of the superstitious gossip of the island, Mr. Wiltshire. Are you a religious man?"

Wiltshire is gazing at the beach. He does not answer, but takes his pipe from his mouth and blows a mouthful of smoke out to sea.

Case: "A pity. They are all Wesleyans here, or Baptists."

Wiltshire: "And you?"

Case: "Ah! I was brought up in the Church of England; at school I became a pantheist; at the University I embraced Buddhism, Confucianism, and the daughter of tobacconists; in my early manhood I was a pious Satanist, and celebrated the Black Mass from Tunbridge Wells to Honolulu; now, in my wiser years, I have married a Wesleyan Samoan native who secretly worships a shark, and am untroubled by faith or doubt. Shall we go to my house first, Mr. Wiltshire?"

As he speaks, the boat nears the beach. Boys and girls dive into the water and swim, calling and laughing around and under the water, a shoal of gay and dark-skinned fishes. The swimmers fling wreaths of leaves and flowers into the boat.

The boat draws up on the beach of Falesá. Car-

17

rying their wreaths, Case and Wiltshire step ashore and walk through the crowds, who ceremoniously make way for them, up the beach toward the village. The village street is paved with grass, through which the lizards run and the small rat-like dogs with their smooth, shining, speckled hides.

The people of the island follow, laughing and singing. They pass under the coconut palms and the towering breadfruit trees, with their scalloped leaves, where the native houses, of bamboo thatched with palmetto leaves, stand. Behind them now, are the sounds of the surf and the sea fowl. Snow white birds fly above them. They walk under flowering acacias, hibiscus and magnolias, under lime tree and shaddock.

The aged of the island stand at the doorways of their huts. One tall and powerful man stands alone under a tree. His chest and face are intricately tattooed.

Case: "He is Tahuku, the wizard."

Children high up in the coconut trees laugh and cry out when a wind shakes the branches. They have shaved heads and topknots.

The younger men wear loinclothes, and some of them have ornaments in their ears and necklaces of teeth. Some of the older men wear robes of white tapa.

The women, in bright robes and dresses and

kilts of printed materials, wear necklaces and girdles of flowers, leaves, and blossoms about their temples and around their ankles. And some of the young girls wear, behind their ears, a single white bud or an hibiscus flower.

Outside one house, a very ancient person, male or female it is impossible to say, lies on a mat in the sun.

Case: "There is a proverb 'The coral waxes, the palm grows, but man departs.'"

Case and Wiltshire walk on through the village decorated for the festival. High above them range the dense woods. Streams run through the valleys. With the sound of the surf is mingled the sound of cascades and waterfalls and the birds of the woods.

One old man of much dignity is smoking a pipe outside his house. He smiles and bows. His luxurious beard is tied in a sailor's knot.

Case: "His beard is worth a hundred dollars."

Only the little brown children trot after the two white men as they leave the center of the village behind. The men and women stand in the clearing under the trees, looking after them.

From the group of trees on the other side of the village comes a young native girl. She is young and slender and light in color. Her eyes are large, luminous and melting as are the eyes of all Polynesians. She wears no festival garlanding or decoration, but only the common dress of the village. Her body, her long black hair and her bright dress are shining wet from the sea or the streams.

Wiltshire sees her, and Case sees that Wiltshire sees her.

Case: "That is Uma."

He darts a quick look at Wiltshire, and the two white men walk on. The children, who calling and laughing, have followed them from the beach, stop suddenly at the sight of Uma and go no further. Uma walks past them, away from the center of the village.

Now Case and Wiltshire approach a large dilapidated bungalow in a clearing a little way from the village and at the edge of the thick, encroaching bush—an unpainted, unmended, weather-beaten board house with a rickety veranda. As they come nearer, a Negro comes out onto the veranda, clad as is Case, in striped pajamas and panama; but, unlike Case, his clothes are untidy, tousled and creased as though he had slept in them. He is an enormous Negro, with a wide, white, face-splitting smile. He raises his panama at the sight of Wiltshire and Case with a friendly, or insolent, flourish.

Case: "The *second* of your three 'white' trading rivals, Little Jack."

Case and Wiltshire climb up the steps to the veranda.

Little Jack: "Good day, Mr. Wiltshire."

He slurs the word so that it sounds like "Welsher." Wiltshire looks sharply at him, but his great sliced melon of a smile is without guile. Wiltshire looks at Case as Little Jack steps aside and lets the two white men enter.

Case, politely: "Oh, yes, we all know your name."

Case and Wiltshire go into the living room of the bungalow. It is dark inside after the bright sun, and it is darker when Little Jack, following Case and Wiltshire, blocks up the doorway onto the veranda with his great bulk. Little Jack stands there smiling as Case, with a gesture, says: "And your third white friend—to be."

Slowly, as his eyes grow accustomed to the light, Wiltshire makes out the details of the room. The windows are shut and spattered with flies dead and alive. Flies are buzzing everywhere. The roof is low and dark, stained with lamp smoke. Three unmade beds lie on the floor against the furthest wall. In a corner, on the floor, lies a litter of pans and dishes. There is no standing furniture. And in the middle of the room, squatting native fashion, sits a pale and bloated old man, the flies thick around and upon him. A bottle stands by his side. He is naked to the waist.

Case: "Captain Randall, the Father of the island."

In the store or trading room of Case's bungalow, there is a dusty counter and on it an old pair of scales. Of the ordinary South Sea trading goods, there is only a meager show, and much of that stained, moldy, neglected: some tinned foods, biscuits, hard bread, cotton stuff. But there is an excellent display of firearms and liquor.

Little Jack leans against the counter smoking a cigar, cleaning a gun, a glass beside him. At a table sit Case and Wiltshire, drinking. A pack of cards is strewn across the table. There are bottles empty and half empty. The table in front of Wiltshire is white with cigar ash. Wiltshire is sitting loosely in his camp chair, his clothes awry, his hair tousled. Case is immaculately sober.

The door between the store room and the living room is wide open. Old Captain Randall is still squatted on the floor, his bottle in his hand.

Case, affectionately: "Dear Daddy Randall! Observe, Mr. Wiltshire, that flyblown old grogpot guzzling and sousing there, and reflect!"

Randall: "Leave . . . me . . . alone."

Case: "Once he strutted and swaggered in all the bars of the South Seas, a bibulous and magniloquent dandy; cut a fine figure at the consulate ball; laid down the law on club verandas; commanded a ship; had a mouselike adoring wife in Auckland and three fine daughters."

Little Jack: "Arabella, Amanda, and Rose."

And Little Jack bursts out laughing in his deep, black voice.

Randall: "All . . . dead . . . all . . . dead . . ."

Case: "And three wives in Tahiti. How are the mighty fallen!"

Wiltshire: "What happened to him?"

Case: "I think he fell into bad company."

Suddenly from outside the veranda, there is a hubbub of native voices.

Case: "What a pity you do not understand the language! You miss so much! Such an expressive tongue! And the intriguing names! Do you know that in Falesá there is a perfectly harmless old gentleman called 'Drinker of Blood'? And another called 'Not Quite Cooked'? Then there's 'Die out of Doors' and 'Bat's Breath' and 'Father of Cockroaches' and 'Dead Man.' "

Suddenly Case pushes aside the empty bottles on the table and says contemptuously: "Dead men!"

Case thrusts a half-full bottle in front of Wiltshire: "Drink, drink to our new friendship. May we both, as rival traders, load the necks of the natives with trinkets from Birmingham. May we drown them in bottles of polecat scent. Let us sell them tinned crab till they walk sideways. May they gulp plum jam till they pop. And in return: let them sweat till they bleed making copra for the pretty gentlemen."

He raises his glass: "I give you—the pretty gentlemen!"

He and Wiltshire drink. Case looks around him, his lip curled in a sneer, at the occupants of the smoky room—Wiltshire, tousled, dishevelled, his face blotched with drink; Little Jack, huge, immobile now, leaning and looming at the counter; Captain Randall, in the dusky near distance, squatted like a big drunk frog.

Then Case inches forward on his chair, conspiratorially nearer to Wiltshire, lowers his voice, narrows his eyes: "You're going to be lonely in Falesá. Even with Little Jack around, and Little Lord Fauntleroy over there—" He nods in the dim direction of the Captain. "—And me. There comes a time when a man needs other company than men."

Wiltshire: "I like my own company."

His speech is truculently blurred.

Case, slyly: "Oh, but not always . . ."

Wiltshire: "I like my own company because I don't object to anything I do." He speaks with the mulish monotonous logic of the drunk. "I'm tolerant about myself. I let myself do anything I like."

Case: "*She* would let you do anything you like as well."

Little Jack's black voice speaks suddenly with relish from the counter: "And if she don't—tickle her in the teeth with a boot."

Wiltshire looks at Case and Little Jack, drunkenly puzzled: "Who d'you mean?"

Case assumes an air of innocent surprise: "Why, Uma, of course, who else?"

Wiltshire: "Uma? Uma? Who is Uma?"

Case, very softly: "—That all her swine commend her—"

Little Jack: "She pretty enough to eat."

Case: "I pointed her out to you as we walked through the village."

Little Jack licks his chops as though he has just eaten: "Yum yum."

Case: "Why don't you marry her?"

It is early evening. In the far background is the chanting of native voices. It is one with the sounding of the surf. It is as impersonal as though it were a happening of the weather.

The table is laden with bottles. The men are as before. Wiltshire's handsome, reckless face is set in drink and stubbornness. The blackness of Little Jack's face merges into the shadowy darkness. Captain Randall cannot be seen at all though the door between the two rooms is still open.

Wiltshire: "No. That's the end of it. I don't want to hear any more. I'm used to living alone, I like it alone. I don't want your girl."

Case: "You admitted you *admired* her."

Wiltshire: "No. She was only a girl coming out of the trees, going by. I hardly caught sight of her. I wouldn't know her again. I never said a word about her."

Case, softly: "I saw your eyes."

Wiltshire: "I don't like native girls. I like being alone. I like being silent. If I want to talk, I can talk to myself, not a lot of pidgin English either."

Case: "Uma's father was a white man, a gentle-man, though a remittance. She speaks excellent English. And Uma's beautiful."

Wiltshire: "All right, all right, she's beautiful, she's pure as snow—and damned dark snow at that —she's young and clever and charming. She's every-thing you say, but why should *I* be *married* to her, *you* tell me that."

Case: "Oh, there's no harm in the marriage."

Little Jack: "I'm the chaplain!"

The sudden, deep interjection is startling, com-ing out of the dark corner where the Negro stands almost unseen.

In the distance the chanting continues.

Case: "When we met, I said to myself, 'Now here comes a stranger—a delightful stranger—to our little community on this earthly paradise. Let us at once offer him all the hospitality a man well needs: drink, and a woman! The drink is, I assure you, the best available. Why not say the same for the woman?"

Wiltshire drinks. Case leans closer, across the table, to Wiltshire, his voice lowered: "Think of the long, hot, loveless nights alone on this little lost island. Alone in your dull, dead room, listen-ing to the silly sea. All alone and nowhere to go in the wide world, no one to care if you sleep or weep or die, no one to care, no one to touch—all the long, hot hours of the night. Uma is beautiful. In your arms she'd be lying still and secret and safe, burning under your mouth."

Wiltshire drains his glass, staring, without seeing, in front of him. Case rises softly, and says in a whisper: "I'll put up the banns—immediately."

He goes out on to the veranda, followed by Little Jack grinning. They go down the steps into the chanting evening. Between them, in the village, men and women move under the trees and around the bamboo houses. There is the sound of the surf.

ᕬ

Wiltshire is still at the table, still sightlessly staring, his empty glass in his hand. And suddenly he hears Randall's voice: "Come . . . here . . ."

And Wiltshire spins around in his chair, towards the open door between the two rooms. He rises unsteadily, and lurches towards the door. He peers down through the semi-darkness and sees the squatted, obese, Buddha-like figure of the Captain. The tall, broad figure with its unruly hair leans, towering, over the old man.

Wiltshire: "Yes?"

There is the continuous buzzing of flies. The flies crawl over the badger-grey bloated body of the old man, but he makes no attempt to brush them off. He looks up at the tall figure leaning over him. Occasionally he moves his hand across his eyes, as though wiping away a mist or cobwebs. He speaks wheezingly slow and slurred. His speech is disjointed; his mind wanders; now he is sly and confidential; now tearful, maudlin; now again there is an ancient remnant of dignity about him; now he is bestial, sunk in stupor.

Randall: "Who are you? I don't know you. You aren't Johnny Adams—or Underwood of the eye—or anyone I know. Johnny Adams's gone. The rest they're dead. And all my beautiful daughters . . ."

Wiltshire: "My name is Wiltshire."

Randall: "I know you now. I heard them talking when they thought I was asleep. They thought I was asleep because my eyes were closed . . . Uma, they said . . . I always sleep with my eyes open."

Wiltshire: "Who were *they?*"

The sight of the old man so rotten with drink has done something to sober Wiltshire.

Randall: "Him and the black one."

Wiltshire: "What else did they say?"

Randall: "Uma . . . I'm sly when I'm drunk . . . I sleep with my eyes open . . ."

Wiltshire: "What else?"

Randall: ". . . so that I can see what I am dreaming. You mustn't think I'm always drunk, sir. I can play the fiddle like King Nero. I can put Master Mariner to my name. Now, what's gone and what's coming, it's all one. Will you try some Randall's Cure? Randall's Cure for Cholera, Toothache, Shingles, Herpes, Hives, Witlow, Boils, Bunions, Nails in the Boot, 90 per cent alcohol . . ."

As he raises his bottle, he brings out his thousand-times repeated joke, he wheezes with a kind of senile glee, then suddenly stops. His voice lowers: "Mind your step. Mind the dark. Look behind you in the sun."

Then suddenly he spins round where he squats, with a squeal. Wiltshire, leaning at the jamb of the door, straightens sharply.

Randall: "Look out!"

Suddenly an old native woman scuttles into the room through a curtain of beads at the far end. She is hideous. Her face is tattooed. Parts of her head are shaven, but also long strands of seaweed-like hair crawl down to her shoulders. She is dressed in black shrouding to her heels.

Randall makes the sign of the cross, but the old woman takes no notice of him. She crosses to Wiltshire. She raises one skinny arm and takes his hand in hers. She mumbles over his hand, strokes it against her tattooed cheek. Out of her lips comes a thin, reedy song. Then again she purrs and mumbles over his hand.

Wiltshire: "Fod God's sake!"

He tries to shake his hand free as he would from an animal that had its teeth in it, but she will not let go. Wiltshire, quickly: "What the hell's she want? What do I do? Cross her hand with silver? Who is she?"

Randall: "Faavo."

Wiltshire: "What's she saying?"

The old woman's voice rises again into a kind of song.

Randall: "I—don't—know."

He has shuffled across the room to a corner and is squatting there terrified.

Wiltshire: "Tell her something. Tell her to go away. Tell her to get on her broom."

But with her long claws she still clutches at his hand; she still mumbles and sings, still rubs his hand across the hideous markings of her face.

Then they hear Case's voice, sharp, hard, imperative. He speaks in the native tongue. Faavo drops Wiltshire's hand and runs, with a strange half-dragging, half-scuttling movement out of the room through the curtain of beads.

Case is standing in the doorway just behind Wiltshire, who has not moved.

Case, politely: "The old lady has taken quite a fancy to you, Mr. Wiltshire. Will you drink?"

Wiltshire: "No. No more. I don't like the hag. She's got claws like a lobster's. She smells of graveyards."

Case: "My dear sir, *what* a way to talk about your future mother-in-law!"

෨

Case is playing his concertina. Captain Randall is playing the fiddle. The tune is a strange yet recognizable version of the Wedding March. They are sitting, playing, at the bottle-laden table.

Wiltshire stands in the middle of the room, a glass in his hand. Near him, holding a book, stands Little Jack. He wears a clergyman's dogcollar of stiff white paper. They are both looking towards the open door leading to the veranda, beyond which can be seen the tropical starred night.

Uma comes in from the veranda, into the lamplit room. She comes in gravely and shy, her eyes looking down. She wears her bridal dress: a kilt of fine tapa, silkenly swathed; a necklace of white flowers; flowers behind her ears; a woven garland on her head a mantle of tapa tied in a bow on the left shoulder, leaving the right shoulder bare. Her feet are bare, but her ankles wound about with flowers. She crosses, and stands between Wiltshire and Little Jack.

Wiltshire moves a few steps towards her. His eyes are hot and reckless. For the first time she raises her eyes to his. She does not smile. Her eyes are beautiful and trusting.

Case and Randall stop playing. Randall fortifies himself with a swig from a bottle at his side. Little Jack begins the "wedding ceremony." Case allows himself, gently, sardonically, to smile.

Shyly, seriously, attentively, Uma listens. Wiltshire looks at her. As the "ceremony" continues, he glances at Little Jack with an expression of distaste, then looks again at Uma who is confident and tranquil. And Little Jack's voice, black, mellow, deep and unctuous, goes on throughout: "Dearly beloved. . . . Those whom God hath joined let no man put asunder . . ."

Uma and Wiltshire join hands. The music of fiddle and accordion begins again; this time, gay South Sea music, but with the fiddle apt to shrill and scrape erratically. Little Jack hands a rolled paper with a bow round it to Wiltshire, who puts it in his pocket. Little Jack smiles his great sliced-melon smile.

Case and Randall are still playing. Randall is

trying to raise his bottle to his mouth at the same time as he scrapes away on the fiddle. Case is smiling.

Outside Case's bungalow, Wiltshire and Uma walk toward the village, hand in hand. The village is pointed with little fires under the trees. The music of fiddle and accordion dims into the background.

In Case's bungalow, Little Jack and Randall convivially are passing the gin bottle one to the other, Little Jack rolling his eyes, nudging Randall, making the mock gesture of prayer, then slapping his thigh and doubling up with laughter; Randall tittering and winking. Case still plays on the accordion, not noticing the drunk antics of the two others but gazing fixedly out at the night beyond the veranda, smiling crookedly, thin-lipped, to himself.

Outside Wiltshire's bungalow, Wiltshire and Uma are walking on under the trees toward their house and their marriage night. There is the sounding of the surf and the dim village chanting.

Wiltshire and Uma come into the moonlit bedroom of Wiltshire's bungalow. He strikes a match, lights a lamp. There is a bed in the corner. Uma looks around her calmly. Then she puts out her hand to Wiltshire. He moves towards her, but stops as she says: "Please!"

He looks at her uncomprehending.

Uma: "Please! For me. The little paper he gave. My wedding paper."

Wiltshire, softly: "No, no."

Uma: "Always I want to keep it."

And she smiles, beautifully, trustingly. Slowly, he hands her the paper. She holds it to her, standing near the table on which the lamp is shining. She looks up at him: "Now I am your wife forever."

He catches her in his arms. The paper falls on to the table, near the lamp. On the lamplit paper in copper-plate writing, are the words:

> This is to certify that Uma, daughter of Faavo of Falesá, is illegally married to Mr. Wiltshire, and that Mr. Wiltshire can send her packing to hell whenever he pleases.
>
> John Blackamoor
> CHAPLAIN

Wiltshire's bungalow looks fresh and clean in the bright, morning sunlight. Wiltshire comes out on to the veranda, smoking a pipe. He leans and looks at the village, at beach and sea. Uma is singing somewhere inside the bungalow.

Wiltshire: "Good morning, Falesá."

White-clad village women, with little dark children in their arms or held on their shoulders, like the women of Gauguin, go down to the sea. Wiltshire: "Good morning, sweet ladies."

And Uma still sings within. Wiltshire speaks lazily, leaning against the open door: "Uma, what are you singing? What is the name of the song?" But Uma sings on, happily, and does not heed him. And lazily he continues, as though he did not expect her to answer: "I think it's a song about love and—waterfalls and—wonderful golden girls and—coral seas and flowers and—lying about in the sun. Uma, I'm hungry."

And he turns and goes indoors. The veranda of the bungalow has three doors opening on to it. One door leads from the store, the other from the bedroom, the third from the living room. Wiltshire now goes into the living room.

The windows are open to surf-sound and sun. There is a table laid for a meal in the center of the room, and an oil stove in a corner. Uma turns from the stove.

Uma: "It is ready." She has about her, always, a sureness and an innocence; she speaks calmly, unhurriedly; she moves with unself-conscious grace.

Wiltshire sits down at the table.

Uma: "I have cooked meat and rice. I have used sugar and salt." She comes to the table, lays down dishes, pours liquid into a cup. "There is breadfruit, and coconut milk to drink."

He follows her with his eyes about the preparation and serving of the meal. There is an air of puzzlement about the way his eyes follow her. He speaks without thinking. All he can do is to look at her. He cannot make her out, or himself.

Wiltshire: "Food for kings and queens!"

Uma: "My song—it has no name at all. It is about love and waterfalls and sea and flowers. It says: Once there was a young man, Karnoonoo, he was very pretty, very rich, and he had many mats, but he wanted an umbrella to give to his wife. The uncle of his wife had an umbrella, and so Karnoonoo hit him on the head with a club and took the umbrella. And everybody was happy."

Wiltshire: "Except the uncle of his wife."

And Wiltshire takes a mouthful of the food. As he chews it, an expression, first if incredulity, then of horror comes on his face. He speaks in a spluttery and strangled voice: "Uma, Uma—for hell's sake! What is it?"

Uma comes near him, much concerned: "Meat and rice."

He lifts half a coconut shell to his lips, and gulps.

Uma: "I make it tasty."

She crosses and goes to a shelf on which are various small tins and jars, takes some of them in her hands. "I put in all the nice things you bring." She puts the tins and jars before him.

Wiltshire: "Curry powder, paprika, ginger, mustard, horse radish . . ."

Gingerly he touches his tongue with the tips of his fingers as though to feel if it is still there. "Lucky I didn't bring any moth balls." Then he laughs and takes Uma's hands in his: "You're the best girl in the world, Uma."

For a moment, his forehead wrinkles into puzzlement again. And he murmurs as though to himself: "That's funny, I *mean* it." Then he shakes the puzzlement away and smiles, friendly, frankly at her: "What's it matter if you can't cook? Let's have breakfast done South Sea style." And he kisses her.

Rather sadly, she takes away the meat and rice as he begins on the fruit.

Uma: "My mother is a good cook."

Wiltshire looks up at her in alarm: "Like you?"

Uma: "Better. More tasty."

Firmly he points a finger at her: "You cook."

※

In the living room of Wiltshire's bungalow, Uma and Wiltshire are setting up home, putting up ornaments and trinkets, bringing out some of Wiltshire's treasures and arranging them about the room.

Wiltshire takes out his treasures one by one from a case, and hands them to Uma. He takes out a little framed picture of a cottage, an almanac type, roses round the door, ivy on the wall, smoke curling from the chimney, unlikely birds flying over the thatched roof, sinking sun. There is a motto underneath. Uma looks at it carefully.

Uma: "What do the words say?"

Wiltshire: "They say: 'There's no place like home.'"

Uma: "This was your home, in England?"

Wiltshire: "Well, no, not exactly. I was born in Liverpool. But I've always wanted to live in the country." Defensively, "It's a very pretty picture."

Uma: "Very pretty. Where is the veranda?"

Wiltshire: "No veranda."

Uma: "All houses have verandas. Where do you drink gin in the evenings?"

Wiltshire: "You don't drink gin in the evening, in a cottage."

Uma puts up the picture, on a nail: "All white men drink gin in the evening—on verandas."

Wiltshire, firmly: "You go to a pub, and you drink beer."

He fishes out another framed almanac picture, an English country inn, much romanticized; smocked gaffers sitting on a bench outside, quaffing from tankards; a jovial, rubicund host in shirt sleeves standing at the doorway; a hay wain coming down the lane.

Wiltshire: "That's a pub. And those old fellows, they're drinking beer. Or cider. I want to keep a pub when I get home."

Uma: "This house, this is not home?"

Wiltshire, awkwardly: "Oh, home's in England, Uma."

Uma: "Home is in Falesá, for me."

But hurriedly, so that he will not notice what she has said, or the way she looks at him, he goes on: "I want to have a pub just like that—with a sign on a tree. I always think about it. I know just what it looks like, where you keep the barrels, the shape of the taproom the snug behind the bar, the benches and settles and the table for dominoes and—I don't know what I'm going to call it. Perhaps I'll call it the South Sea Arms or Trader's Rest or just The Red Cow, perhaps, like the one in the picture."

Uma: "I like the Red Cow best. I have never seen a cow."

Wiltshire: "It's a kind of animal that gives milk."

Uma: "Like a coconut?"

Wiltshire: "Yes, like a coconut, only it's got four legs and a tail."

Uma lost her momentary sadness. She laughs: "A coconut with four legs and a tail. Oh!"

Wiltshire: "And it makes a noise like 'moo.'"

Uma, laughing, unbelievingly: "The coconut that has four legs makes a noise like 'moo.'"

Wiltshire: "And their husbands are called 'bulls.'"

Uma: "The coconut has got a husband now. Oh, damned fine!"

And they burst out laughing. He takes various other treasures from his case: a little drawing of a Victorian woman.

Wiltshire: "That's my mother."

Uma: "Does she cook how you like?" Piously: "May God rest her soul."

He looks at her in surprise. Then he fetches out three books.

Uma: "You read?"

Wiltshire, shaking his head ruefully: "I'm not the reading sort. I've always been too busy, and too—wild. I'm a black sheep, Uma—no, don't ask me what a sheep is, you'd only laugh. That's a Home Doctor, and that's a Ready Reckoner, and that's—"

Uma: "That's a Bible."

Wiltshire, awkwardly: "I never put much store by that." He nods toward the picture of the Victorian woman, now hanging over the mantelpiece. "She gave it to me." He brings out various pieces of sailor's junk from all over the world: a Birmingham Buddha, shells, little fake figures, a china mermaid, at which Uma looks with approval.

Uma: "Very pretty. No legs."

He brings out a big brooch. "For you. You pin it here." He touches his chest.

She pins it to her breast, looks at it admiringly.

He brings out a clock, winds it, makes it chime.

Wiltshire: "Like Big Ben."

Uma looks at it with respect as though it were a foreign god, carefully puts it on the mantelpiece.

Uma: "Big Ben!"

He brings out an old, weighted, fat-bottomed

children's toy, scratched and faded, that sways drunkenly backwards and forwards, never toppling.

Wiltshire: "That's a Kelly." The Kelly lurches back and forth.

Uma: "Kelly! Kelly!" And she laughs again. He laughs at her with a loving smile, as she watches the drunken doll.

ℛ

In the store room of Wiltshire's bungalow, Uma and Wiltshire are setting the store to rights. Cases, barrels, chests, are nearly all tidily stacked. The trading goods, the tinned foods, the sweets, rice, biscuits, etc., are arranged on the shelves. There are large jars of salt. On the counter are bales of cotton goods, rolls of printed material draped as in a provincial English store, cheap trinkets, ribbons and ornaments, beads and brooches, some umbrellas and panamas. Rolls of matting are propped against the counter. Uma is sweeping the floor with a broom of twigs.

As Wiltshire works on, he talks, quite casually to Uma, who as casually answers him: "Uma, why did you come and live with me?"

Uma: "Mr. Case, he told me you loved me."

Wiltshire: "I didn't know." He lifts a heavy case, stacks it behind the counter. "I didn't know I did." He begins to move the contents of the case on to the shelves. "But I do."

And they both go on tidying and preparing the store.

At last Wiltshire stops and looks around him, at Uma, at the heaped goods, the merchandise waiting: "All spick and span! Just like my grannie's shop back home except there's no sherbert and toffee apples." Ceremoniously, "I declare this store open."

He crosses the room, flings the door wide, hearing the sounding of the surf. Uma at his side, he looks out at Falesá, at the green of the village dotted with coconut palms and breadfruit and houses. All over the village, men and women are stalking, silent, wrapped in their robes, like Bedouins in Bible pictures.

Then he goes out on to the veranda. He pulls a chair near to the store room door, sits on it, tilted back to the wall of the bungalow. Complacently, he lights his pipe. "And now we wait for custom."

Uma disappears indoors.

Wiltshire: "Roll up, you beautiful ladies of Falesá! Come on, you elegant gentlemen!" He cocks an eye at the sun, high in the cloudless sky.

Wiltshire is still sitting in his chair on the veranda. He looks at the sun. It is lowering down the sky. Still, the villagers move among their houses and the trees, but no one approaches the bungalow.

Wiltshire, calling: "Uma! Uma!"

Uma comes out onto the veranda.

Wiltshire: "Trade's brisk. We're doing fine! Nobody's come. Nobody all day. This rate I'd better enlarge the premises."

Uma: "In Falesá they are silly people."

Wiltshire, in exasperation: "What do I care! They can stand on their heads and *howl* to the moon so long as they trade. They can crawl backwards and bark like sea lions so long as they *buy* and bring copra." Perplexedly, "What's wrong? Why don't they come?"

It is early evening. Case is seated on the steps of his veranda, a knife and a piece of wood in his hands. Expertly he is working the wood to a smooth surface. Below him stands a group of villagers, among them the tall, powerful, tattooed native, Tahuku, the wizard. He is talking in the native dialect. The other villagers nod vigorously and loudly assent to what he is saying. Occasionally, Case, not looking up from his carving, puts in a word in native, a word that sets Tahuku off again.

Behind Case, can be seen, through the open door of the trading room, Little Jack selling merchandise to village women.

The talk of Tahuku and the natives grows in volubility and excitement. Case fans the flames every now and then with a few words. There is a shout, and Case turns his head to see where it comes from.

Coming towards the bungalow, out of the encroaching bush, walks a young, handsome native of a noble and dignified appearance. Behind him, laden with baskets of copra, come his men. Case rises to his feet. He addresses the young native in the dialect, then repeats in English: "Salutations, Maea."

And the young native, Maea, inclines his head in greeting.

Case with a gesture of the hand and a word in dialect, dismisses Tahuku and the rest and goes down the steps to Maea. He walks side by side with Maea, followed by the native bearers, toward a shed at the side of the bungalow and unlocks it. It is half full of copra. The natives carry their loads of copra into the shed.

Case, calling: "Little Jack!"

Little Jack, smiling, comes down the veranda steps. Case nods his head towards the copra shed and the new load of copra. "Weigh it up."

Little Jack goes into the shed, puts the copra, load by load on a great scale. Maea and Case stand watching him. Little Jack calls out the weight of each load, and Case makes a note of it. And Maea answers. It is clear that they are haggling over price.

It is evening and the moon is shining. At Wiltshire's bungalow there is the sound of sad, insistent chanting. Fires are lit before some of the native houses among the trees. Wiltshire stands rakishly at the door of the store room, a glass in his hand.

Wiltshire: "Come on, you misbegotten ladies! Roll up, you monkey gentlemen, roll up! Everything for sale! You bring your copra and you take your choice! All bargains here! Tinned pork and marbles! Cough drops and calico! Combs for the bald 'uns!"

His voice is slurred and excited: "Plug tobacco for the babies!" Suddenly he tosses the contents of his glass over the veranda. "Oh, what's the matter?"

He slumps down in a chair, and looks at beach and village, moon, sea, stars: "Tomorrow is another day. You'll come tomorrow."

And all the time in the background is the sad chanting, the insistent accompanying rhythmic handclapping of the villagers by their night fires. Uma comes out on to the moonlit veranda.

Wiltshire: "Sit down by me, Uma."

But she stands a little away from him timidly.

Wiltshire: "It's all right, love. I'm not angry. Never with you. Tomorrow everything'll be fine and dandy. I'm staying off the drink, Uma, I mean it. Cross my heart, I'm not goin' to be another old man Randall. I've drunk in every doghole and shanty under the sun. I've done things I don't like. Nobody'd like. I've lived ugly. Never no more. I want to stay quiet now. Here with you in Falesá."

Uma puts her arm around his shoulder.

Wiltshire: "Uma, why do they sing like that every night? Are they sad?"

Uma: "No."

Wiltshire: "Are they happy?"

Uma shakes her head slowly: "No."

Wiltshire: "Why do they sing, then?"

Uma: They always sing at night."

Then they are silent. The sea sounds on the beach. The voices are chanting.

श

Outside a village hut there is a circle of natives around the fire, some distance from it, clapping and chanting. Nearer the fire is a smaller circle of natives, Tahuku, the wizard among them. Tahuku is talking animatedly. His listeners nod.

လ

At a stream in the early morning, some dozen young men, young women, and children sit silently in a half circle, wrapped in their clothes. They are quite still, all staring in the same direction. There is a boulder in the middle of the stream, and on this sit, draped and silent, two native boys. All are silently staring in the same direction at Wiltshire's bungalow.

A curl of smoke rises from the chimney. There is no sound, not even of the surf.

Inside the bungalow Uma is singing; in the bedroom, Wiltshire, bare to the waist, is shaving with a cutthroat razor before a mirror, across which is lettered, "Kennedy's Battle Axe Gin."

Wiltshire, calls out: "What's *that* song about?"

Uma goes on singing, softly, from another room. Wiltshire dips his face and head and hair in the tin basin, comes up spluttering. He speaks as he towels: "*I* know. Somebody cracked his aunty

50

with a frying pan, and they all lived happily ever after."

He pulls on a shirt.

Uma is sitting at an old-fashioned English sewing machine, working it with patience, incompetence, and childish curiosity. She is singing to herself.

Wiltshire calls to her from the other room: "Do you know what day it is today? It's *tomorrow!* It's like I said. It's the day when everything's going to be fine and dandy."

Uma sings softly on, but looks, for a moment, as he speaks, sad and troubled.

Wiltshire: "You'll see! We'll have all the bucks of Falesá prancing in with their little topknots bobbing and buying away like billyho."

Her troubled expression deepens. He comes in, in white shirt and ducks, washed, combed, shaven. She looks up at him.

Wiltshire: "And all the belles in our bright new dresses, la-di-da as peacocks—"

Ever so slightly Uma shakes her head, but Wiltshire does not notice. He goes out of the living room on to the veranda. His walk is buoyant. Suddenly he stops at the sight of the silent starers each side of the stream, some way from the bungalow, the little, robed, silent, staring boys on the boulder in midstream. They are all staring toward the house.

But the crowd is greatly increased. The far bank of the stream is lined for quite a way now with standing figures. Perhaps there are so many as thirty men and women, and many more children. There are two half circles of villagers, each side of the stream, and behind the farthest half circle, a still, standing line of them, graven images.

It is a dead-silent, dead-still gathering, who stare directly and unwaveringly at him. Wiltshire moves a step toward the rail of the veranda. He speaks softly, subduedly, to himself, though his lips do not move. The little interior monologue is many-mooded and laconic.

Wiltshire: "Looks like people at a wake. Who's dead around here? It isn't me. I can still taste breakfast—pepper and bluebottle, ugh! What d'they want? Saw a crowd like this once, in Haiti—but then a trader was thrashing his wife indoors and she was singing like a cat. What've they come to watch? They've had a dekko at me before, plenty of times—all very civil and smiley. I might as well be on the scaffold here, and all these citizens come to see me hang."

He moves down a veranda step, stops still. There is a movement among the grave, graven children at the front of the gathering, as they turn, for a moment, to speak to one another. But he does not hear their voices, and, the next moment, they are unwinkingly still again.

Far behind the farthest unmoving line of standing starers, a few village women, white and scriptural, move, or seem to glide in the quivering sunlight, serene and unperturbed about their business.

Wiltshire moves down another veranda step, staring all the time at *them*: "Maybe it's an old island custom. Make a stranger feel at home. Go and sit and stare at his house for a couple of hours. Make him feel good. Give him the horrors." Now Wiltshire has reached the bottom of the veranda steps. "They're waiting! Yes, that's what they're doing. They're waiting for something to happen! To *me!* Fire from heaven burn me, bones and baggage! Thunder and lightning! The earth to open and—gollup me up! Maybe they want me to subscribe to the football club! Why don't I get Case here? He'd laugh at me, all smug and sly. Why don't I call Uma? Frightened to show I'm frightened. Nothing to be frightened *of!* Speak, or move, or laugh, or something."

During this he has begun to walk, very slowly, towards the silent watchers: "All right, I'm coming your way."

As he approaches the first half-circle this side of the stream, there comes from the watching crowd a low, indistinct murmur of voices, an undercurrent and spreading whisper of sound more like a muffled and mumbled prayer than anything else. He comes nearer. To cross the stream he has to pass close to three little boys at one end of the first half circle, three boys wrapped in their sheets, with shaved heads and topknots. They dart quick glances at each other as Wiltshire comes near, but stick their ground, unnaturally still and solemn.

He comes nearer, and the murmur of the gathering dies. It seems that, passing the three small boys, he must touch them. And suddenly there is a wink and gulp of terror in their faces. One of the boys jumps up and is off like a flash, squealing. The other two jump up and try to follow but fall together to the ground, tangled in their sheets. In a second, they slip out of their sheets and flash off naked. And among the watchers, who have not moved, there is a sudden, quick bark of laughter.

The two boys on the boulder in the middle of the stream sway, as though in a gust of wind. Then silence and stillness again.

Now Wiltshire walks slowly past the silent, unmoving starers. Silence. An old woman moans, a moan of piety and superstitious horror. From somewhere in the crowd comes one high strangled cry of invocation or of warning.

Silence.

Wiltshire walks on. The watchers do not turn their heads as he goes by. Only their bright eyes follow him, then again stare directly ahead.

And Wiltshire is striding across the green of the village, leaving the gathering behind. Under the breadfruit trees and palms he goes, past empty nouses, their black-eyed doors open, and unattended fires. He talks to himself as he goes: "It frightens a man to be alone. To know that there is nobody but himself. It frightens a man to be alone, and not to be sure he *is* alone. But worst of all, it frightens a man to be alone in a mob and not to know what they are doing or why, and when nobody will tell him at all."

He is walking down a grove of trees. Behind the trees is the sea. There is the noise of the surf. Canoes skim the water. On the beach are parties of fishermen by lighted daytime fires; fishermen by their canoes at the edge of the surf; fishermen in the sun lying asleep in their canoes fetched up on the sand.

And walking up the grove toward Wiltshire comes a white man, short, very fat, wearing a cassock and galoshes, and carrying a down-at-spoke umbrella. The two approach each other on the narrow path. Wiltshire's face lights up eagerly. The face of the fat little priest is very dirty, benign, and affable. Wiltshire strides eagerly toward the priest. The priest waddles toward Wiltshire. They stop. They are both smiling.

Wiltshire: "Good day to you, sir."

And the priest answers, courteously, rapidly, most amiably, in native.

Wiltshire: "My name's Wiltshire. I'm the new trader here. I'm mightily glad to see you."

And the dirty, fat, good-humored priest with

the woebegone gamp and the splay galoshes answers in French. And the eager light on Wiltshire's face is fading.

Wiltshire: "Don't you speak any English?"

Priest: "Engleesh?" And in French, rapidly, he says that unfortunately he is not fluent in that language, but will try. "I am Father Galuchet." He bows. "They call me—Father Galoshes."

He looks down, with a smile, at his galoshes.

Wiltshire speaks now a little too clearly and loudly, as though he is speaking to a child or a deaf person: "There's something happening here I can't understand. I need your help."

He wears a puzzled, almost pleading expression, which the priest at once understands.

Priest: "I can help you?"

They are walking together now, through the grove and back toward the village by a different way than that already taken by Wiltshire.

Wiltshire: "Oh. Oh yes, you can help. I want all the help I can get. Look here, Father, the only other white man I can ask about this is Case—"

At the name "Case" the priest stops, his face sparkles with animation through the dirt and whiskers, he gestures violently and excitedly: "Ah, Case!"

He speaks rapidly in French to the detriment of Case's morals, antecedents, companions, and physical, spiritual and eternal prospects. Then, suddenly,

56

with a word and gesture of apology, he breaks into English, slowly: "In Falesá he is an evil man. The natives, they are children. They do not comprehend. They do not purpose to harm. But he—"

Again, his anger and indignation overcome his English and he flows into denunciatory French, describing the immoral and unholy activities of Case, bringing himself up short with: "You have heard of M'sieur Johnny Adams?"

Priest: "Ah, he is run away. He is full of fear. He run as though the devil chase him. And that is true."

The priest crosses himself as they walk on again, through the grove toward the green of the village. Again, the priest races into French, saying that Case has frightened Adams off the island with spells and devilish tricks. Then he breaks once more into English: "This Case! *He* drives Johnny Adams from Falesá. He makes spells, calls up evil spirits. He makes him mad with fear until he screams at his own shadow. Johnny Adams scream all night because of what he sees—terrible voices and faces. It is Case who drive him mad until he run away."

Wiltshire: "How do you know? How do you know it was Case's doing?"

Priest: "Do not ask me that. I *know* as there is a God above. Be careful, my friend. Case does not want *two* traders on Falesá. That is why he frighten poor Johnny out of his head till he go."

Wiltshire: "I'll be careful, I'll be careful of what I can understand. I only want to know one thing now—why don't they trade with me? Why don't they *come?* Why are they sitting there in front of my house? Like mummies in the sun, all dumb and still?"

The priest shakes his head in bewilderment. He answers in French that he cannot understand. Now they are nearing the green of the village.

Wiltshire: "You'll see for yourself in a minute Explain *that* to me in French or double Dutch or—"

Wiltshire flings out his arms. He and the priest have come to the edge of the green, from which they can see Wiltshire's bungalow. There is no crowd before the bungalow. Not one man, woman, or child remains. A few villagers move, without looking at them, serenely about the houses under the trees. There are sea sounds. Birds fly. And the priest looks up at Wiltshire.

Case is sitting on a step of his veranda, indolently carving a little head out of wood. The door of the trading store is open. Little Jack is in the store, a cigar in his mouth, serving some native customers. There is the soft babble of their voices.

Wiltshire: "Trade's brisk."

And Case looks up and smiles as Wiltshire comes up.

Case: "You find it the same? The store thronged, the ladies haggling and dickering, the copra house choc-a-bloc? Have some gin?"

Wiltshire: "No to both questions. No gin, and no trade."

Case: "The Falesán native, Mr. Wiltshire, is an inveterate Tory. That is why he worships the dead. He sticks to the Old Firm. The coming of a new trader is a radical event—like a dropped aitch in the Carlton Club—or a demand for stout and winkles at the Royal Garden Party. You are new. You are eyed with misgiving. You must allow them time."

Wiltshire: "This morning I found half the village squatting on its backside, staring at my house. They didn't speak. They didn't move."

Case: "You see? Oh, the cautiousness of these cocoa-colored diehards!"

Wiltshire: "They looked at me like people look at a leper. Or a man with a curse on him. It seemed like they were praying."

Case: "Before I knew the language, I thought they were always telling *me* Polynesian limericks."

Wiltshire: "They've got some sort of jinx on me. They won't come near me. They won't trade or speak."

Case, ironically: "What *could* you have done? Blasphemed their ancient gods? Robbed their temples of precious jewels? No, no. That happens only in the duller fairy stories."

Captain Randall, sodden, obese, shuffles on to the veranda through the living room door. He makes a few feeble efforts to catch, with his hands, some invisible spots and presences that dance before him. Belches, and flops down in a rickety cane chair by a table on which is a gin bottle and an ancient gramophone. He pours himself a shaky drink.

Case, casually: "The savage chiefs of Tonga could cure a man of his liver by *touching* him with their feet. They would have to dance the cancan on Daddy Randall."

Wiltshire: "What do you know of the French priest, Case?"

Case rises, his knife and carving in his hand: "He takes snuff. He doesn't wash. He has worn the same cassock for thirty years. It could conduct a service by itself. I knew you had been talking to him. Falesá is all eyes and ears. Did he tell you that I had scared Johnny Adams off the Island?"

Wiltshire, slowly: "I gathered he believed that."

Case: "Poor Father Galoshes, who never washes! Did he tell you *I* drove Johnny mad?"

Wiltshire nods.

Case: "I had no need to drive him mad, I can assure you—even if I had been so inclined. What would a pack of old wives' tales, a turnip-head and a lantern do to a man who lowered majorams of wood-alcohol down himself like the buckets of a dredger? Father Galoshes has been in the Islands so long he has turned native: his mind is full of dark mischiefs, tribal murders, sorcery, diablerie, fetishism, taboo."

Wiltshire: "I'm tabooed all right. And there's a real solid reason. Sane as a ship's biscuit. I'm going to find out. I want to talk to the Chiefs, to the Elders, to whoever-it-is. I'm not going to go round like a madman with a bell, ringing it to let them know I'm coming. I'm not a bogey man to frighten children. And I'm not frightened of bogey men either."

Case: "There's a pow wow in the Speak House tonight. I can take you along—I don't *swear* that they'll listen."

Now from the veranda comes the tinny scraping of an old gramophone record.

Wiltshire: "They'll listen. They're going to listen, cannibals and Baptists, vampires, Wesleyans, the whole tabooing swarm of 'em."

His face is hard and set. Case looks up at him with shrewd, appraising eyes. On the veranda Captain Randall sits by the table and the gramophone. The hoarse record is playing "Stick to the Ship," a Victorian sea ballad. Tears are running down Randall's cheeks.

℞

That night there is a large crowd of villagers, men, women and children, outside the Speak House. They are clustered around the doorway; standing in thick, chattering knots; peering in at the windows; everywhere noising and pressing. Suddenly a warning is hissed and rippled among them.

They all turn away toward the sound of a gabble of new voices. The mob at the doorway opens. Hedged about by young village men, none now in their trade clothes but in the native dress and ornament of important occasion or celebrations, Wiltshire and Case appear in the opening made by the crowd. And the sound of the crowd rises, animated with anger. The young guards press back the crowds.

Wiltshire and Case walk together into the Speak House. Inside, in the center of the room are the five chiefs. They sit on mats. Each has a fan in his hand, a fan plaited from young leaves of the coconut tree.

One is clad in pajamas. His cruel face is tattooed. He is soddenly corpulent.

One very old and puckered chief, in the center of the group, wears elegant, painted shoes.

One of the young chiefs, handsome, proud, is clad in white kilt and jacket. He has a very intelligent face. It is Maea.

One of the chiefs is Tahuku, the wizard.

Before the chiefs, two other mats are spread out.

As Wiltshire and Case enter, the old chief with the shoes motions them to sit on the two mats. Case and Wiltshire sit. At the open doorway, the crowd, still hissing, chattering, murmuring, cranes and jostles to look on.

The old chief with the shoes speaks first, in native. As he speaks, the chief in pajamas hands round to the others, excluding Case and Wiltshire, a large plug of ship's tobacco. Some put a piece in their pipes. The others put a piece in their mouths. The old chief stops speaking.

Wiltshire: "What's he say?"

Case: "They wish you good morning."

Wiltshire: "Took a long time."

Case: "Also that they are ready and willing to hear your complaints."

Wiltshire: "Tell 'em."

And Case, in native, addresses the House. When he stops, there is silence.

Wiltshire: "Tell them I've come to do them good. Tell him I've come to bring them trade and civilization."

Case speaks. The old chief with the shoes answers, in native.

Case: "He says they have quite enough civilization, thank you. They have more guns, gin, and disease than they know what to do with."

The old chief speaks again.

Case, in a whisper: "I sold him those shoes. He only wears them for celebrations and important meetings. He's very proud of them. Every time he wears them they cripple him for a week."

Wiltshire: "Tell him I bring no guns, or gin, or disease. I come to do honest trade."

And Case addresses the House again. At one of his remarks the old chief looks disapproving, but the chief in pajamas laughs out loud, nudges his neighbor, looks with lewd, moist eyes at Wiltshire.

Then Tahuku speaks. The crowd at the door, which has been very softly murmuring throughout, now becomes utterly quiet. But, as Tahuku speaks, the crowd suddenly moans. All together. Angry no longer, but grieving and fearful.

Case, whispering: "It's a bad business."

Wiltshire, grimly: "Ask them why I'm tabooed."

Again, Case speaks, very briefly. Maea answers, in native, but he is stormed down indignantly by the others.

Wiltshire: "Tell them I'm a regular trader. I trade for copra. I pay a fair price. If what they want's a present all round, I'll do that. Clothes or food or—"

A few words from Case. A few words from the chief in pajamas, who makes play with his eyes and moistens his full lips. As the chief in pajamas is speaking, Case whispers to Wiltshire from the side of his mouth.

Case: "A perfect gentleman—when drunk."

Wiltshire: "What's he now?"

Case: "Sober."

Then Maea speaks again, a few words.

Case: "Maea does not want bribery."

Then Case nods in the direction of the chief with the pajamas: "That joker's name is 'Prince Born Among Flowers.' He says the only present he really wants is a human hand."

The chief in pajamas winks.

Wiltshire, quite loudly: "I want to know why the village bars me. What have I done to them? Get a straight answer, can't you?—Gabble, gabble, gabble—"

Case speaks again, in native. There is a hubbub of argument from the chiefs. Then the old chief with the shoes raises his hand. There is sudden silence. The old chief speaks.

Case touches Wiltshire's shoulder: "Come on. The palaver's over."

They both rise. Case bows to the chiefs. Wiltshire does not bow. They walk out, Wiltshire going first. As Wiltshire goes through the doorway, the crowd about it shrinks away on either side of the door without a word. The villagers press and jostle against each other, so that nothing of them, their bodies or their clothes, will touch them. They do not make any sound at all, not even the littlest children.

Wiltshire's back is to the crowd, his shoulders set. Case is talking to him with hardly veiled irony: "You should have bowed, ceremoniously."

Wiltshire: "I bow to no one."

Case: "It made a bad impression."

Wiltshire: "I don't aim to impress. I wanted the truth. What is it?" And Wiltshire turns and faces Case. "Tell me!"

And Case's voice changes: "They won't have anything to do with you. They're frightened of you."

For the first time, Wiltshire looks amazed: "Are you crazy?"

Case: "*I'm* not. It's they who won't go near you."

Wiltshire suddenly laughs, but with no humor: "Lord, am I that ugly?"

Case: "It's *they* who are ugly customers."

Wiltshire, bitterly: "No customers of mine."

Case: "I can't make it out. There is some superstition so deep, so dark, I can't get hold of it at all. It's secret and it's very old, and it's nasty."

Suddenly, Case takes Wiltshire's arm and walks away with him toward the bush climbing from the end of the village. From somewhere in the distance drums are beating. They walk toward the noise of the drums. At the edge of the bush, the drum noise loudening, Case stops and says: "I have never warned you. Look out for the beach of Falesá. Watch your step. Do not trust one of these outwardly Christianized and civilized islanders! (I except your dear wife, a treasure among women.) Inwardly, they are as savage as their grandfathers. And their grandfathers!"

Case and Wiltshire are coming to the edge of the grove. Through the trees they see a squatted company of natives round their fires. The drumming comes from the center of the company.

Wiltshire: "What's that?"

Case: "A parish meeting."

Wiltshire: "Why have you brought me here?"

Case: "On similar occasions, not so very long ago, Mr. Wiltshire, the chiefs, girdled with the hair of dead women, would come with their drummers, dancers, girls, and priests. And up to them would be brought the very red baskets—of long pig. Long pig! Human meat! And the poor relations would take home their tidbits in Swedish matchboxes."

Out of the company of the squatted and drumming islanders rises one young man. He begins to dance.

Case: "Oh, the naughty grandfathers And the grandmothers too! They had a very sweet tooth. And there are their grandchildren, drumming and dancing on the same blood-stained ground. Beware of them. The souls of the dead haunt the bush. They rise up out of the ground like butterflies. They are like mist. You walk into them, and you vanish, you are dispersed. They worship the serpent, and the crab, and the eel. And Harpies more beautiful than any woman, who sing like turtles. The ghosts of beautiful women always fly backwards so that you cannot see the worm marks on their faces.

And there are cannibal ghosts. The living eat the dead, and so the dead must eat the living. The ghosts tear out the eyes of the living, because the eye is always sweet and dainty. Yes, *those* are the things they believe. Never forget that. What is sacred is dangerous. It is dangerous to interfere with death. Now you know why I could not interfere when Johnny Adams died. I had no wish to run foul of *them*."

All through this they have been moving up to the company around their fires. The movements of the young boy dancer have grown wilder and more sensual with the quickening of the drums. Other dancers join him, leaping out of the company, out of the bushes, to the barbaric drum music with savage whirling and turning.

ॐ

There are some opened cases of dress material on the counter in the trading store of Wiltshire's bungalow. Uma is wearing a bright, store flowered dress, short and cut low. There is a ribbon in her hair, a cheap bead necklace round her throat. Her cheeks are rouged, her lips painted. She has a looking glass in her hand. She is holding some of the dress material across her shoulders, admiring it in the glass.

She tries another length of material, holds it across her breast, examines its effect, head on one side, then lifts up another roll of printed cotton from the counter. She hums a song to herself and makes the little movements of a dance. And Wiltshire comes in. His face is grim, his eyes burning. He snatches the material away from her, thrusts her aside.

Wiltshire: "Get that dress off you. And those beads. And that doll's ribbon. You look like a slut from Papeete. I'm no drunken sailor with a month's pay in my pocket. Scrub that slime off your face."

Uma is standing still and upright, looking directly at him.

Wiltshire: "Here's the whole damned Colney Hatch of an island turned against me, wriggling away like I was dead and rotten to the eyes, gaping and moaning, and all you can do is daub yourself up and mince round this pigsty like a geisha girl with the itch!"

Still Uma does not move, or turn her cool, sad gaze from his.

Wiltshire: "Why aren't you cooking those meals of yours—they'd make a Kanaka mongrel vomit? Why aren't you playing tunes on your pretty sewing machine? Why can't you speak?"

He comes nearer to her, very near, his eyes wild, his voice harsh. But she does not flinch.

Wiltshire: "Or don't you speak to me either? I'm taboo. Did you know that? I'm taboo. I frighten people. Do I frighten you? I'm taboo. I'm a leper. I'm doomed, I'm damned. I give the children fits. I turn the coconut milk sour. Listen to me, my wife! Can you tell me something? Just one little thing. That's all I want to know. One little thing. Why am I taboo?"

And now Uma's expression changes. Through Wiltshire's abuse and mockery she has remained outwardly unmoved, taking his temper unflinchingly, almost with pride. Now she looks at him in amazement. He poise is forsaken. Her hands go to the low-cut top of her dress, as though she were shielding nakedness.

Uma: "You do not know? You do not understand?" Softly, "Oh, God help me now." She looks at his eyes. Her trace of a smile is almost compassionate. "It is me. The taboo belongs to me."

And she turns and goes into the room behind the trading store. Wiltshire does not move, but stands there, lost, awaiting her. And she comes back, into the store. She has changed her store dress for the everyday white dress of the island, plain, ungarlanded. She has wiped away paint and rouge. She walks across the store to the veranda door, her head high. Wiltshire watches her, a dawning comprehension in his eyes—that, and love. At the door she turns toward him.

Uma: "I must go now. I am ashamed before you. All the time I thought: he knows. He knows it is me, all the time, all the time. And he does not care. He loves me. He does not care."

Wiltshire comes to her. He stands quite near her, does not touch her, looks, simply, at her as though for the first time. He speaks as though he is himself surprised by the inevitability of what he is saying: "And I don't care."

Uma: "I must go now. You see, when I am gone, people will come. Everybody will come because I am gone. The taboo has gone. You will have copra. You will be rich."

Wiltshire, slowly: "I don't care about the taboo, now. Not now. Nothing matters except you. I would rather have you than anything under the sun."

And, slowly, he puts his arms around her.

ॐ

It is night and there is a moon. Wiltshire is sitting on the floor of the veranda, his back against

Uma: "It was Mr. Case."

Wiltshire: "Mister Case, that's the only good turn you'll ever do me in this life."

Uma: "He brought us here. We were on Falealii. He gave us a house."

Wiltshire: "And then? Then he made love to you, the little gentleman with the big words—"

Uma: "No. I said 'No.'"

Wiltshire: "No, Mister Case. And then?"

Uma: "He went away. And one day nobody speaks to us. They take up their mats when we go to church and go away. Nobody will speak. But girls shout after me. You will get no husband. Forever and ever. All men are afraid. It was *talo pepelo*. A lie. *You* came. *You* were not afraid. *You* were not ashamed of me. *You* married me. Oh, I love you too much."

And Uma and Wiltshire kiss.

Wiltshire, softly: "Tomorrow I see Case. Tonight, we sleep." They rise and go indoors.

From the bungalow can be seen the village. But all the village is not sleeping. Out of the moonlit trees, in little separate groups, silently come natives who take up their positions opposite the bungalow, the other side of the stream. In their white robes like grave-cloths, they sit and stare.

It is the beach next morning, the surf, the reefs, the sea, the canoes far out, the birds wheeling high. Palm trees cast shadows on the sand. A group of little girls is seated, singing, on the beach. Suddenly they stop singing. And the smallest girls reach out to touch with their hands the hands of the others for protection. Wiltshire is walking along the beach, looking all about him. He takes no notice of the now silent girls. Determinedly he strides on. He strides across the shadow of a palm tree on the sand. We look up at the palm tree. And suddenly the fans of the palm part and there, at the top of the tree, sits a native boy, motionless as an idol. He has his hand held searchingly above his eyes. He is looking out to sea. And then he waves and waves, calling: "Misi! Misi!"

And the voices of the little girls on the beach take up his cry, waving out to sea. Wiltshire, striding along the beach, stops and stares out to sea at the sound of the shrill young voices. There is a long whale boat, painted white, coming toward the island. Twenty-four paddles are flashing and dipping in the sun. And all of the crew are singing.

Wiltshire walks on in the direction of the part of the beach directly below the village. Many children are running down from the village toward the approaching boat. Far behind them comes Case. Wiltshire sees the distant figure of Case and hurries on toward him.

Case stands on the beach looking at the boat nearing the island. The crew's singing rises. Astern of the boat is an awning and under it sits a white man. Villagers run past Case, from their houses, from the groves, to the beach and boat. Noisily and waving, children skip and prance at the edge of the surf. Case watches them with a cynical indulgence, hands in pockets.

Wiltshire, from behind Case: "Turn around." And Case whips round.

Wiltshire: "Take your hands out of your pockets." Case makes no move. And Wiltshire hits him hard across the face with his open hand.

Wiltshire: "Now will you take your hands out?"

Case edges his hands out of his pockets. One hand slides toward his hip pocket. Wiltshire grasps the sliding hand and twists it savagely. A knife drops on to the sand.

Wiltshire: "Remember last night? You said the taboo on me was secret and nasty. I know how nasty now. I know the secret now."

76

Case is apparently not listening to what Wiltshire is saying. His hand is stroking his cheek, on which Wiltshire's blow is still burning. Case speaks very slowly, from between tight-drawn lips, with a kind of venomous shocked surprise: "You hit me!"

In the background is heard the shrill calling of the children.

Wiltshire: "Because Uma wouldn't let you put your dirty claws on her, you had her tabooed. You poisoned the villagers with some baby-scaring trash about Uma so that they wouldn't have anything to do with her, so that they were frightened of her."

Case makes a move to pick up the dropped knife, but Wiltshire, in a second, has his foot on Case's hand. And Wiltshire picks up the knife and tries his finger along the edge.

Wiltshire: "Oh, I believe your Father Galoshes now. You scared Johnny Adams off the island with the same mumbo jumbo you used on Uma, didn't you?"

He takes a step nearer Case: "Didn't you? I think I should cut your tongue out. And then you 'married' me to Uma so that your taboo would work on me as well, so that there wouldn't be *two* traders on this Island. So that you could get all the copra. Didn't you? And you thought I'd be a lily-livered skulker too, like Adams, and slink off? Oh, no, not me. I'm staying. But first of . . ."

And Wiltshire draws back his fist. Now the air

is loud with the salutations of villagers and the clamor of children. The white man is getting out of the boat at the edge of the surf. He is dressed in white duck clothes, with helmet, white shirt, and tie. He carries a white sunshade. The children dance about him in delight, but suddenly there are cries from the villagers.

The white man looks up from the children at Wiltshire and Case fighting. Wiltshire knocks Case to the ground. Case rises unsteadily and is floored again. He lies where he falls, in the sand, and Wiltshire stands over him. The white man moves toward them. The villagers make a path for him. He hurries up. As he nears Case and Wiltshire, Case kicks Wiltshire in the side.

Stranger: "Stop!"

Wiltshire turns round, his face savage, and confronts the stranger with brutal truculence: "What do *you* want? D'you want to see me kick him in the fangs?"

But Case has risen and is moving off, his eyes fixed with hatred on Wiltshire. At Wiltshire's words and the tone of his voice, the still crowds gathered behind the stranger begin a suppressed but angry murmur.

Stranger: "Who are you?"

Wiltshire: "I'm Wiltshire. I'm the new trader here. And who the hell are you?"

Stranger: "My name is Jenkins. I am a mission-ary."

His voice is liltingly Welsh. His face is stern.

Wiltshire: "You look like one. Come on, I've got a job for you."

Missionary: "Have you now indeed?"

Wiltshire: "And I want two of your crew as well."

Missionary: "Do you now? Would you like my boat too?"

Wiltshire: "I'm not asking any favors. I don't like favors, and I don't like missionaries. This is the sort of job you've got to do whether you like it or not."

Missionary: "You don't like missionaries, Mr. Wiltshire? And I don't like drunken bullies. It's your kind that's fouling the Islands. It's you and the guttersnipes like you that *dare* to sell my people drink and drugs and teach them your own vices. I see the people here know you only too well. They keep away from you. Wise boys!"

Wiltshire: "I'm not drunk, Mr. Missionary. And don't you worry about *them*. I'm taboo. I'm the devil."

Missionary: "Indeed? I've always wanted to meet you. How is business in Falesá?"

Wiltshire: "I'm not to be made fun of by . . ."

Missionary, interrupting: "Not even by a missionary? Such feeble old fellows we are too, not a spark of fun in us."

Wiltshire: "I want you to do something for me. I want your help."

Missionary: "That's better talk now."

Wiltshire: "Because you're the only person who can help me. Will you come with me? Please."

Missionary, dubiously: "Well, I *may* be wrong about you. I'll take a chance."

The missionary turns and calls out in native to his crew. Two of them join him. They are powerful men. They scowl at Wiltshire. The missionary steps up to the side of Wiltshire, and together they walk up the beach. The two native crew walk close and protectively behind.

Missionary: "Where are we going?"

Wiltshire: "To my place."

ॐ

Now the missionary and Wiltshire, closely followed by their guard, are walking up the steps of the veranda of Wiltshire's bungalow and into the trading room. In passing, Wiltshire quickly, so quickly that it is scarcely possible to see what he is doing, tears a brass ring off the thin blind on the window

They walk through into the living room. Uma is there. The missionary takes off his pith helmet. Tufts and little thickets of wiry white hair spring out from the sides of his head, like hair on a clown's head. His white eyebrows are jutting and very thick. Beneath them his eyes are bright and black, missing nothing.

Missionary: "Why, Uma, my dear! Well, well!"

He addresses Wiltshire: "We are old friends." Uma curtsies. The missionary looks from Uma to Wiltshire and then back to Uma.

Uma: "*We* are husband and wife."

Wiltshire: "Uma, give us your marriage certificate."

Uma puts her hand quickly to the breast of her dress.

Wiltshire: "Come on. You can trust me."

He puts out his hand, and trustingly, but reluctantly, Uma brings out her marriage certificate from the breast of her dress. She hands the paper to him.

Wiltshire turns to the missionary, looking at him squarely: "I was married to Uma by Little Jack the black man. You know him?"

Missionary: "Badly."

Wiltshire: "This certificate was written by Case. Do you know him too?"

Missionary: "For my sins. And for his."

Wiltshire: "Then you can guess what's in it?"

Missionary: "I can."

Wiltshire: "And now I've found that Uma is tabooed. Case saw to that because he couldn't have her for himself. And so long as I'm with her, I can't trade here and the curse is on me too. All right, I understand that. So this is what I am going to do."

And Wiltshire tears up the marriage certificate and scatters the pieces on the floor.

Uma wails out: "Ave! Ave!"

She begins to clap her hands and cry with grief. Wiltshire catches hold of her hand.

Wiltshire: "And this is what I want *you* to do. Marry us properly, with ring and witnesses and everything."

In Wiltshire's open hand is the brass ring he has torn off the window-blind.

ॐ

In the living room of Wiltshire's bungalow, Wiltshire and the missionary are sitting at the table, the remains of a meal before them. The native witnesses have gone. Uma brings over to the table a teapot and two cups and saucers which she lays before them. She pours the tea as the missionary speaks: "Mr. Wiltshire, I have to thank you for a very lovely pleasure. I have rarely performed the marriage ceremony with more grateful emotions."

He takes a sip from his cup, then lifts a bushy, white inquiring eyebrow at Uma: "Is this tea?"

Uma, standing near, waiting for appreciation, nods her head.

Missionary, to Wiltshire: "I shouldn't really be in these parts till the rainy season—it comes down in buckets, worse than Wales. I haven't been home for forty-three years and seven months—but I've been hearing strange stories about Falesá."

He takes another sip, looks at Uma: "Are you sure this is tea?"

Uma nods again: "I made it from the packet."

Missionary: "It must be me who tastes of salt, then. It's queer how you hear these rumors flying across from island to island. After a long time you begin to *see* them almost, like puffs of smoke coming over the water. You *feel* there's something strange and wrong somewhere, in the way your boys sing as they row when you're out in the mission boat.

Wiltshire lights a cigar.

Missionary: "I heard stories too, mind, about Johnny Adams with the club foot going so sudden, scared off the island, so they said, but I knew there was strangeness blowing before I heard a word. And then, when I stepped off on the beach . . ."

Wiltshire: "You were right. There's strange things happening, and I'm not so far off knowing why."

Missionary: "Tell me all you know."

Uma raises the teapot and is about to pour.

Missionary: "No, no, no more tea!"

And the missionary bends forward to listen, his eyes bright under the white eyebushes, looking keenly at Wiltshire and at the glowing end of his long cigar.

Wiltshire puts his fingers to his cigar to take it out of his mouth. The cigar has burnt down to the end.

Wiltshire: ". . . and all the rest, I *guess*."

Missionary: "Case is a bad enemy. You were wrong when you said *you* were the devil hereabouts, Mr. Wiltshire. He has a very clever representative on the island already."

Wiltshire: "And he gives himself the devil of

a lot of trouble too, just to be the only trader and get all the copra there is."

Missionary, slowly: "I wonder if that is all he wants." The missionary rises from the table. "Now you leave the taboo to *me*. I'll show these backsliders what for. I'll give them a sermon from First Kings, 19, that'll wither 'em in their pews. I'm the only man in the world who can use the Welsh hwyl in Polynesian dialect. And I'll see Case too."

He collects his pith helmet and parasol. Uma comes, shyly, into the room. He gives a little bow to her: "Thank you for your hospitality, Mrs. Wiltshire."

And he shakes Wiltshire's hand and goes out. On the veranda steps he opens his parasol, holding it above him. He hurries off toward the village, a slight, old, indomitable figure.

℘

The missionary is standing outside Case's bungalow. The doors along the veranda are closed.

Missionary, calling sternly: "Come out, Mr. Case."

And Case's voice answers mockingly from within: "Come in, Mr. Jenkins."

The missionary goes up the steps. He is about to try to open the door of the trading store, when the door, as though by itself, swings open. The missionary enters. He walks into the trading room, stops a little way inside the threshhold, his parasol still up. The door closes.

Case: "An open umbrella indoors brings bad luck."

The missionary lowers his umbrella, closes it, his sharp eyes staring under their spiky bushes into the darkness, from which Case's voice comes lightly and banteringly.

Case: "That's better. We are all superstitious here. We never look at the new moon through glass. We never look at the new moon. We believe in omens, auguries, wizards, werewolves. We wave wands and rub rings. We fee faw fum in the night. We say our prayers. We cross our fingers. We touch wood."

Throughout the missionary grips his parasol as though it were a sword of righteousness.

Case: "And here's an old salt we throw over our left shoulder."

Out of the darkness, keeping his back to the wall, Captain Randall sidles into the trading room, his eyes owl-blinking in the light. He stops, his back to the wall, his eyes on the missionary. Behind the missionary looms Little Jack at the veranda door. The missionary takes no notice of either, but speaks, fearlessly, into the dark.

Missionary: "Come out here in the light, where I can see you, Mr. Case."

Case: "Come on into the dark, where *I* can see you, Mr. Jenkins."

And from the darkness a macaw screams.

Case, soothingly: "Pretty poll! Pretty poll! His mother was frightened by a missionary."

The missionary moves across to the door leading to the dark: "Come out here, or by God, I'll come to you."

He raises his parasol menacingly.

Suddenly there is light in the living room, bars of muted light across the floor. Case stands now at the open shutters. He wears white trousers, but is bare to the waist. Around his neck are hung native necklaces of sharks' teeth and little bones. His feet are bare. His arms and chest are intricately and hideously tattooed all over, not with sailors' flags and anchors, names, serpents, arrowed hearts, but with tribal signs and caste marks.

Case: "Come to me, if you must." And the missionary enters the room. He stares at Case, his bright eyes hard and unwavering.

Missionary, softly: "Very nice, very nice. I should have known."

Case: "You with your sun-brolly and your Bible,

your tracts and your gimcrack chapels, spreading your message over the islands like a bucket of white-wash, hymning and ha-ing, what could *you* know?"

Missionary: "So you have turned savage."

Case: "I was savage from birth."

Missionary: "You must have been a very nasty baby."

Case: "I was Caliban's son brought up for the church. I was a child suckled by wolves, brought up to brush my fangs and wash my paws before meals. I was a savage brought up to say 'sir,' respect my elders, kowtow before the law, learn to read and write, suffer the classics in a rathole for the sons of gentlemen, proceed to hallowed university, take a worthless degree . . ."

The missionary shakes his head slowly and rue-fully as he looks at Case. Case ironically attitudin-izing, full of disgust and venom there in the fly-loud, fly-blown, bottle-strewn bedded room, his hand at the barbaric ornaments around his neck, the tribal signs, the painted eyes, the exotic tattoo-ing clear on the brown of his arms and chest.

Missionary: "A B.A. too."

Case: "Enter a profession, marry a decent woman, increase the population, achieve prosperity and ulcers, die respected in bed . . ."

Missionary, softly: "I wonder where you *will* die—and instead, you're chief cook and bottle washer on a tiny South Sea island, trying to teach a handful of natives to be naughty."

Case: "I teach them to be evil."

Missionary: "Go on with you man, I've no patience. Evil is powerful. And you—you are nothing but a sick little moochin picking the wings off bluebottles."

Case: "Oh, my turbulent priest, you are scoffing at me now. You are belittling my bad deeds. I admit quite frankly to you that my opportunities for doing harm here are very small. I could achieve far more were I on the Government of a Great Power. But I do my best."

Missionary: "You make up some story or the other about a young girl because you cannot seduce her, and she is tabooed by the village. You pair her off with a newcomer, so that he cannot get any trade. What lies did you tell him about the other trader, Adams, to get rid of *him*? How did you frighten *him*?"

Case: "Oh, that was simple, even for an amateur diabolist. He has a club foot, you see. I told the chiefs and elders that he wore that ungainly boot because his foot was cloven. After that they would have nothing to do with him. And then he drank till he saw blue devils. And then he ran away. And only *I* was left."

Missionary, in disgust: "You're a fraud, Mr.

Savage Case. Here you are practicing your hellish hanky panky just to keep other traders off Falesá. You profess to love Evil for its own sake—and it's all for profit."

Case: "I want no other trader here because I like the island too much. I want no stranger to share it. This is my island."

Then he speaks with a kind of ironic contempt, satirizing his own romanticism: "I know all the noises and smells of it. I know the beach and the bush and the wild pigs and the duck in the mangroves and the beetles on the vine and the smell of bats in the trees. I know the cries of all the birds in the haunted bush and every chime of the surf; acacias, magnolias, hibiscus, passionflowers pomegranate; the stars of the night fires outside the houses at deep blue midnight; the drums high away up in the forgotten wood; the death songs; the death dance; the temples and sacred groves, huge terraces of stone all peopled with the dead. I love the ancient fear of Falesá."

Missionary: "And, by God, *I'll* drive it out!"

❦

The deep, cracked bell of the Wesleyan Chapel and the high, harsh bell of the Baptist Chapel are ringing. And suddenly both bells stop.

Outside one of the chapels can be heard the voices of the natives singing inside, then the sound of their praying. And then the voice of the missionary raised in passionate exhortation. His voice is punctuated by the dolorous cries and the pious, fearful interjections of the congregation.

In the chapel, the congregation is sitting on the floor on mats. The women are on one side of the long, low room, the men on the other. In the pulpit at the end of the chapel stands the missionary preaching with great eloquence. Maea is in the audience.

The miissonary raises his finger in admonition, storms, warns and wheedles. The congregation responds to his every mood, approving, shuddering, giving little cries or grunts of grief and contrition as he moves them. He speaks loudly the words "Case," "Wiltshire," "Taboo." Maea, sitting in the front of the chapel as befits a chieftain, nods in solemn approval.

Later the natives come out of the chapel. They are all silent. They dare not look into one another's faces. Very slowly, their eyes downcast, they begin in silence to disperse.

The missionary comes out of the chapel. The grieving and humiliated villagers, slowly returning to their homes, to the beach, to the bush, to the green of the village, look away from the missionary in silent guilt and shame.

And then Case, immaculate in white ducks, comes jauntily out of the trees and approaches the missionary. When he is quite near he raises his hand with a dramatic flourish to command attention. The dispersing villagers stop and surround Case and the missionary, still, silent, not understanding them.

Case: "So here is the holy man."

He turns to the villagers and translates his words into native.

Case: "You have been preaching against me but that was not in your heart."

Again he translates the sense of what he has said.

Case: "You have been preaching for the love of God—but that was not in your heart."

He translates again for the benefit of the uncomprehending crowd whose stillness and silence is now compounded of guilt and shame toward the missionary and fear of Case. The missionary does not speak, holds himself firm and erect, his hands steady on his parasol, his eyes meeting Case's with a fierce disdain.

Case: "Shall I show you what is in your heart?"

He turns to the villagers, translates, all with perfect, insolent ease and plausibility. And then, turning again to the missionary, he makes a deft and rapid pass at his breast. Rapidly, professionally, he flashes his hand in the air, opens his hand. In his palm lies a silver dollar. He shows it, flashing it in his hand, before the eyes of the villagers who step back fearfully. A low and terrified murmur spreads through the crowd.

Case: "A silver dollar! Your heart is full of the greed of money."

He translates quickly into native. The word and the news of the miracle ripple through the voices of the crowd, and amazement rolls in their eyes. Case flings the coin to the ground, and those nearest it back quickly away, as though it were a contamination.

Case: "What is your tongue made of?"

And again, pattering in native, he makes a deft and rapid pass about the missionary's mouth, flashes his hand in the air, opens his hand. In the palm of his hand moves a live scorpion.

Missionary, ruefully to himself: "Oh that I had learnt conjuring instead of Hebrew!"

Case flings the scorpion to the ground, and the

crowd in horror retreat from it. And once more, rattling out in native his prestidigitatorial patter, he conjures from the missionary's head a handful of maggots, which he casts from him contemptuously. And the crowd wails. Some of them run away. Some of them, crying out at the prodigy they have seen, hubbubbing with horror, their guilt and shame toward the missionary vanquished by their fear of Case, cluster around him.

Missionary, to Case: "You've won for the moment, with your little parlor tricks. But don't think you'll win for long. I've buried worse scamps than you, Mr. Case. I may do you that service yet."

And he goes off, followed by a small band of the faithful.

Maea has watched the conjuring and the vanquishing of the missionary aloofly from a place on the edges of the crowd, above which he towers. Now Case sees him for the first time, beckons him with a gesture of the head. Maea turns on his heel and walks away, not following the missionary, but alone.

In the store room of Wiltshire's bungalow, all the goods are laid out ready and waiting for the customers who do not come. Wiltshire looks around bitterly at the stacked shelves, the rolls of stuff, the cases, then takes his rifle from a corner, slings it over his shoulder, and goes out. From the living room can be heard the noise of Uma's sewing machine.

Wiltshire walks alone through a grove. He hears, coming from behind a thick flowering bush, the sound of soft and childlike, delighted and delightful laughter, the sound as of children at play. Curiously, he puts aside the ferns and leaves and sees two enormous native women, squatted on the ground, smoking clay pipes. Their high, lovely, childlike laughter dies. They look up at him in horror. And with a wry smile he lets the parted leaves and ferns meet again and goes on through the grove.

Now Wiltshire is walking through bush. He hears in the near distance the snapping of undergrowth, and stops. He unslings his rifle, holds it ready. Silently he moves towards the noise, which goes away from him as he moves. He catches a glimpse of a white panama hat some distance away among the leaves. Very quietly, he follows the hat, then stops.

He sees Case walking away from him down a narrow path that threads among ferns and flowers of a wide grove. Case has a rifle and a sack slung over his shoulder. Then Case seems to disappear, to vanish as if by magic through a seemingly impenetrable wall of bush.

Wiltshire waits some moments, then follows the path that Case had trod. He looks everywhere for the opening through which Case must have vanished. But he cannot find it.

Now Wiltshire is walking through another part of the bush. He comes into a wide clearing. Crossing this, he hears native voices. And into the clearing comes the young chief Maea leading his men, with spears and rifles, on a hunting expedition. Maea gravely salutes Wiltshire in passing. With a surprised expression, Wiltshire watches him go on into the bush.

Wiltshire is walking in a deserted part of the village at dusk, his arm around Uma. There is the sound of the sea. They reach a small dilapidated native house and go in. Squatting in the middle of the floor is Faavo, Uma's mother. A few mats and clothes are thrown across the open rafters of the room. The furniture consists of a keg, a tin box, a straw pallet, some coconut shell cups, some bottles, and a lantern lit. Faavo has a palm branch in her hand. As Uma and Wiltshire enter, she snatches at Wiltshire's hand and kisses it. Uma squats before her, Wiltshire looking down at the two women, one young and beautiful, one old and ugly. But now there seems nothing sinister about Faavo's ugliness, despite her tattooing. She seems a grotesque but amiable old lady.

And suddenly she begins to chant. She knots the leaves of the palm branch in her hand, here a leaf, there a leaf, according to some precise formula. Uma asks her a question in native. Again she chants and twists and knots the leaves.

Wiltshire: "What's she saying?"

Uma: "She is talking to the dead."

Wiltshire: "I hope they don't answer."

Faavo chants on.

Wiltshire: "She can speak English, can't she?"

Uma nods her head.

Wiltshire: "But the dead can't—I see."

Uma asks another question of Faavo, in native, and Faavo answers.

Uma: "She says the dead say you are good."

Wiltshire: "Thanks."

Uma: "She says the dead tell her to trust you. Faavo has twenty cocoanut trees. The dead say she is to give them to you. Then you can make copra."

Wiltshire: "Tell her to tell the dead I'll do them a good turn one day."

And Faavo looks up at him and grins: "You look like my husband, white, very tall. Very pretty. Very jokey. Very nice. Always drunk."

ॐ

In a cocoanut grove in the early evening, Wiltshire, Uma, and Faavo are making copra.

Uma: "All day every day we make copra. Why?"

Wiltshire: "No one will work for us, that's why. We've got to make it ourselves."

Uma: "Why do people want copra?"

Wiltshire: "Because they sell it for money, that's why."

Uma: "But why do *white* men want copra? Do they eat it in England?"

Wiltshire: "You're ignorant, that's what you are."

Uma: "Yes, ignorant all the time."

Wiltshire: "They use it for . . . understand?"

Uma: "Yes. Still ignorant."

Through this Faavo is working silently. They have made all day very little copra.

Outside Case's bungalow the door of the copra shed is open. Maea and some of his men who are bearing great loads of copra stand there. Inside the shed stands Little Jack. Some of Maea's men take in a load of copra. Little Jack examines it, values it, calls out the price to Maea.

Maea: "No."

Little Jack looks up in surprise. He repeats the price.

Maea: "No. Fetch Case."

And Little Jack goes out of the shed towards the bungalow. Maea stands silent, handsome, and aloof among his men.

In Case's trading room, Little Jack talks urgently to Case, who is leaning against the counter, glass by his side, carving a piece of wood.

Little Jack: "Ah don't like the look of it; Maea's been gettin' funny for a long time now. All he said was 'No.' He won't take our price."

Case pockets the knife and the piece of carving and goes out. Followed by Little Jack, he comes up to Maea outside the copra shed.

Case speaks in native to Maea.

Maea: "No, I speak English."

Case, casually: "That's what you think, you noble illiterate hoddy-doddy with your bags of nut meat." In a louder voice, "We give you a fair price. X per Y ton."

Maea: "No. Missionary tell it is not fair price. He say you cheat. You give me Z per X ton."

Case: "I'll be boiled in Battle-Axe gin if I do! You bring me copra, Maea. Same price always."

Maea: "No."

He directs his men in native. They lift up the loads of copra they have placed in the copra shed.

100

They stand waiting for his commands. And he tells them, in native, to go. They carry off their loads.

Maea: "Missionary tell bring you no more copra. Maea obey."

And he turns to go. But Case's voice makes him turn back. Case comes up close to him, his face twisted and evil.

Case, softly: "If you go, Maea, if you take your copra—anywhere else, do you know what will happen? You know that Mister Adams went mad before he ran away, don't you? Do you know why? Shall I tell you?"

And softly, insidiously, he speaks in native. And fear steals across Maea's face.

℧

Wiltshire, Uma, and Faavo are making copra in the coconut grove in the sunlight. Wiltshire and Uma turn their heads as they hear a sudden burst of laughter. Faavo takes no notice, goes on working. Little Jack and a group of grinning native boys are standing some distance off under the palms.

Little Jack, gloating in his deep, black voice:

"It does mah eyes good. See Mr. High and Mighty, boys, working like a black."

And he leads the satellite laughter. Uma and Wiltshire look at Little Jack and the natives. Then they begin to work again. Faavo never raises her eyes from her task.

Little Jack: "Never seen a white man sink so low pick his own copra."

Wiltshire seems deaf to Little Jack's sneers, works on, never looks round.

Little Jack: "Make his women work too. That's lower'n a bush rat. Make his lady wife slave all day in the sun. Mighty bad! Yes, sah, his *lady wife*, married all neat and holy. By me!"

The native boys laugh their toady laughter.

Little Jack: "Better she stay with Mister Case, but he throw her out when he finish—when we all finish, Daddy Randall and me—"

And a juicy, split coconut hits him square in the mouth.

Wiltshire is standing up, his arm still tensed after the throw of the coconut; and Uma crouches fearfully against the palm tree; and Faavo works without heed; and the native boys, awed and excited, hiss among themselves; and Little Jack slowly wipes the splurge of the coconut away from his mouth.

Wiltshire stands ready and waiting, tensed, eager, with that reckless twist to his lips.

Wiltshire, softly: "Now."

Little Jack looks down at his own great hands, almost as though in surprise, and clenches them into fists.

Little Jack: "I killed a man once, with mah hands."

And then his slowness drops off him, and he comes out fighting, springing on the balls of his feet.

Wiltshire, softly: "Now, scum."

And Wiltshire comes to meet him. They exchange heavy, cruel blows to the body without giving an inch.

Uma straightens, holds herself taut, backed against the palm tree. Faavo, squatting, looks up for the first time. The native boys breathlessly inch nearer the fighters.

A blow from Little Jack rocks Wiltshire on his heels. Another blow crashes him on his back. But he springs up and batters in again. At each ramming slam to the body, each pile-driving punch, each jaw-jolting and sledging thump, the native boys cry out avidly, delightedly, with lust and terror. And Faavo runs to her dead. Now Little Jack is basted to the ground but comes up flailing.

And Wiltshire is ready for him, Wiltshire snarling and savage, no hero-who-must-win, but a violent and vicious fighter who never thinks of losing.

The native boys gape aghast, grunt and squeal,

are dancing on their toes themselves and shadow thwacking, as Wiltshire hooks and hammers, and the great, wild cudgeling blows of Little Jack black-and-blue the air.

And Faavo chants to the dead, the old, forgotten words rising and falling to the rocking rhythm of the scienceless, merciless, almost-murder match in the clearing under the palms.

Now the towering Negro slows. Wiltshire hurls in two bloody fistfuls, and the splashed sobbing tower topples. The native boys scream out, come yelling round Wiltshire, seizing his gashed knuckles, waving his hands and their hands, hullaballoing, kicking the fallen tyrant with their bare feet. They dance round Wiltshire grinning, back-slapping, barbaric children, slippery and gay after a blood bath. Wiltshire's bruised lips part in a smile.

It is early evening in a clearing in the bush. The clearing, draperied with vines, is among tall trees, roped with liana, arched overhead with interlacing boughs, among convolvulus, giant creepers, and the late, occasional singing of unseen birds.

Into the clearing comes Wiltshire at the head of a hunting expedition of young natives. They come to a stop in the clearing.

A full stream foams past them, vanishing into dense, descending foliage. Great layers, terraces, of strange, lush bush go down from the eminence of the clearing. And below, the stream foams into sight again, in a wide grove through which one narrow path threads among ferns and flowers and is lost. It is the grove along whose path Wiltshire saw Case walking with a sack over his shoulder, and where Case disappeared so suddenly and mysteriously. Wiltshire sits down cross-legged, the natives circling him. Wiltshire lights his pipe, passes the tobacco among the natives, who put it into their pipes of coconut shell.

Wiltshire, to the circle: "Now we all good friends. Go hunting every day."

First Native Boy: "All good friends."

He puffs smoke with enjoyment.

Second Native Boy: "You hit Little Jack bam bam."

And in delighted pantomime he re-enacts the blows that laid Little Jack low. The others clap their hands, cry with approval.

First Native Boy: "You no frightened of nobody."

Wiltshire looks intently down at the little winding path in the strange grove below. And he points to the part of the grove, the seemingly impenetrable wall of bush where Case disappeared: "No road through there?"

First Native Boy: "One time one road."

Second Native Boy: "Now the road dead."

And a third boy speaks in native: The others nod their heads vigorously, their eyes wide.

Wiltshire: "Nobody go there?"

Again he gestures down.

First Native Boy: "Nobody, nobody."

Wiltshire, softly to himself: "I saw somebody go through there all right. Somebody I know very well." To the natives: "Why does nobody go there?"

First Native Boy: "Too much devil stop there."

Third Native Boy: "*Aitu, aitu.*"

Wiltshire: "Oho!"

Second Native Boy: "Man devil, woman devil, baby devil."

Wiltshire: "Too much devil."

The boys mutter in native.

First Native Boy: "Devil stop there all time, man go there, no come back."

And a murmur of awed agreement rises.

Wiltshire: "You think *I'm* a devil?"

Second Native Boy: "No, no! *E le ai!*"

And the others laugh; laughter of friendship.

Wiltshire: "Uma, she a devil?"

With murmurs of "*E le ai*" they all shake their heads.

Wiltshire: "Why are we taboo then, Uma and me?"

And the murmurs fade. The native boys look abashed.

First Native Boy: "People savvy nothing in Falesá. Man no devil. Man plenty fool all-e-same." Softly, "Devil there."

And he indicates the bush below them. Dusk is growing on apace.

Second Native Boy: "Devil sing in trees, aieee, aieee."

And his wailing imitation frightens all the native boys, including himself, so that they huddle closer and group near Wiltshire for protection.

Second Native Boy, in an awful whisper: "Devil *shine* in trees, go aowoo, aowoo."

First Native Boy: "Eyes in trees go . . ."

And with spread-out fingers he indicates the size of the eyes, and raps and clicks his fingers together to suggest the opening and shutting of big devil eyes.

Second Native Boy: "Dance in trees, shine, sing, I see him."

And he makes with his hands, sinuous side-to-side dancing movements as of a hanged man waltzing in the wind.

First Native Boy: "I see him my own eyes, I hear him sing, I see him *jump* in ground." And his hands jump jack-in-a-box. Suddenly his hands, upraised in pantomime, slap to the sides of his head, a terrified, involuntary movement. He is staring saucer-eyed down the steep gardens and galleries of the bush to the path winding in the grove where the river that passes him comes again into sight. Along the path, out of the eastward tangle of bush, out of the devil-occupied area, the figure of Case can be seen walking in white.

Second Native Boy: "Tiapolo!"

And the word sighs and moans among the native boys.

Wiltshire: "That's Case."

First Native Boy: "Case Tiapolo!"

Wiltshire: "Where did he come from? He disappeared just there last time. Where did he come from?"

First Native Boy: "Tiapolo!"

The figure of Case is lost as the path winds into the high greenwood. And silently the native boys slip into the bush, seeming hardly to stir the ferns, branches, and flowers. Wiltshire alone stands up, looks down at the grove where the path winds, and at the strange, dense, east of the bush. Dusk draws down.

It is almost dark. At the foot of Wiltshire's veranda steps stand two massive native braves. They are both armed. They stand sentinel-still. Wiltshire approaches the bungalow, and stops dead at the sight of the two armed, powerful guards. Still some distance from them, he slips his hand into his hip pocket, brings out a jackknife, clicks the bright blade open. Slowly, knife in hand, he goes nearer the bungalow, ready for anything, his stride the sprung lope of the hunter.

But when he is quite near them, still standing erect and immobile, they part, so that the veranda steps are clear, and lower their arms. Wiltshire goes up the steps, shielding his open knife. As he moves, a man's voice speaks commandingly in native from the veranda. The two guards go off into the gathering darkness.

Half way up the steps, Wiltshire sees that, sitting on a shadowy part of the veranda, are Uma and a native. The tip of the native's cigar is glowing. Uma springs to her feet, comes along the veranda to meet him.

Uma: "Oh, darling, darling, here is Maea."

She raises her head for him to kiss her. He kisses her lightly, his eyes on the still-shadowed native and the glow of his cigar.

Uma: "He has come to speak to you."

Maea stands up. He comes forward to meet Wiltshire. He is smiling, and puts out his hand. Wiltshire clicks his jackknife shut, pockets it, and takes the outstretched hand. The two men shake hands, looking into each other's eyes, sizing each other up.

Uma, Wiltshire, and Maea are at a table on the veranda. A bottle, glasses, and a box of cigars are on the table.

Wiltshire: "You want to trade with me, but you're frightened of Case, that's what it comes down to. Why do you want to trade with me? I'm taboo on the island."

Uma translates. Maea speaks.

Uma: "Maea says he is a religious man."

Maea: "I Bible man. Baptist."

Uma: "The missionary say that Case is wicked. No Bible men to trade with him."

Wiltshire: "Good for Mr. Jenkins. You're the richest man on the Island, Maea, 50,000 coconuts a year. And you want to take your trade away from Case and give it to me. Case won't like that." To Uma: "Ask him why he's frightened of Case."

Uma speaks in native.

Maea: "Tiapolo."

Wiltshire, narrow-eyed, turns to Uma: "Uma, what is Tiapolo?"

Uma: "Devil."

Maea: "Big Devil."

Wiltshire: "How can Case be Tiapolo?"

Uma: "He *belongs* to Tiapolo. He is his son. When he wants anything in the world, Tiapolo make it for him."

Wiltshire: "And you believe that?"

Uma: "I do not know. But he goes into the bush up there—" And she gestures eastward. "Alone, where the devils live. And they do not hurt him. Sometimes he takes the young men with him and shows the devil dancing. They hear him talk to Tiapolo. Tiapolo answers. They hear him sing and cry."

Wiltshire, softly: "And they see him shine."

Uma, in surprise: "Yes. You have seen him sing and shining?"

Wiltshire, grimly: "I'm going to. Tonight."

Uma rises swiftly and comes to his side, imploringly: "Nobody ever go there but him. He has a church to Tiapolo."

Below the veranda, something stirs in the darkness, the shape of a man listening. Uma's voice continues from above. "Nobody ever but him comes back." Imploringly, "You must not go. Please, Mister Wiltshire."

Wiltshire: "Does Maea believe that moonshine? Tell him: If I scuttle this 'devil,' he needn't be frightened of Case any more. Any more ever. If I destroy your Tiapolo, I destroy Case. I'll smash his church and his devils."

Again, the shape of a man stirs in the darkness below the veranda, listening. Wiltshire's voice continues from above: "All the singers and shiners. All the hobgoblins in the east of the bush."

Suddenly the great, dark unrecognizable figure runs off through the darkness.

Wiltshire, softly, to himself: "Though I don't know how." He rises.

Uma: "In the east of the bush is a place called Fanga-anaana. Oh, never go there. Women devils live there. Beautiful. They have bells they ring, and if a man hears them his bones turn to milk."

Wiltshire: "I'll take care of *them* too, bells and milk and all."

But Uma looks at him entreatingly.

112

From above the wide grove in the moonlight, a stream foams out of the descending galleries and gardens of the tremendous, verdurous, impenetrable high interior of the island. It is the grove Wiltshire and the native boys saw when they sat together in a clearing and talked of Tiapolo. Along the narrow, winding path through the grove goes the lithe figure of Wiltshire, bearing a lit lantern. The path is that on which they saw, from above, Case walking out of the dense eastward bush.

Wiltshire reaches the end of the path where it threads among ferns and flowers and is lost. His rifle is slung over his shoulder. He hears the distant sounding of the sea. He forces his way through the thick moonlit vegetation at the end of the path.

Once within, the moon is put out, like a candle, by the windy, swarming, dark draperies of vine, the arches of interlacing boughs, convolvulus, and giant creeper. All sound is muffled and swaddled. His lantern goes on, like an eye before him.

And then he is out again of the thronged and teeming jungle dark, into moonlight and the far, but clear sound of the sea. Before him lies a long mound of stones and great boulders, the beginning of an ancient wall stretching out seemingly endlessly.

There are coco palms, mummy apples, sensitivie and guavas. And all about, the high bush; trees going up like the masts of ships, ropes of liana hanging down, orchids growing in the forks of the trees like fungi.

He goes on, soft-footed, wary now, spying around him. On all sides are to be heard faint and stealthy scurries; the newly unwoken warnings of little, unseen animals; the prying fingering of gusts of wind from the sea, in ferns, leaves, flowers, and shadows. The lantern and the moonlight make the bush all turning shadows that weave to meet him and then spin off, that hover over his head and fly away, huge, birdlike, into deeper inextricable dark. The floor of the bush glimmers with dead wood. The leaves quiver, the great ferns bend and bow, the glimmering deadwood crackles.

And, all at once, he hears a sound of singing on the wind. A high musical ululation that seems to come from many places and many shadows at the same time. The music of the small falling spheres. A wisping and wailing like the tail or wake of a falling rocket. A ghost note rising and

swelling and dying away and swelling again. Some-
one weeping, most beautifully, not of this earth.
A harp, glissando'd by drifting leaves and water.

He stops, unslings, and cocks his rifle. His
eyes range the singing dark, dart this way and that
among wavering shadows, weed and creeper, wil-
lowing trees, articulate wildness. He takes a few
guarded steps forward. Moonlight and lantern-light
show the controlled fear on his face, the sweat on
his brow. He speaks to himself, softly, to keep his
courage up, by challenging the unknown wailing:
"Come on, you beautiful woman of Fanga-
anaana."

And the single undulating ghost note is taken
up by a score of others. The bush is highly wild
with music. Then the wind blows in a sudden gust,
and the leaves before him burst open. He sees a
face in the middle branches. Then the leaves close.
And out of the closed leaves comes the sound of
harping, weeping, and singing. He lays down his
gun and lantern, clicks his jack-knife open, sticks
it between his teeth, and approaches the tree.

Out of the closed leaves comes the sound of
harping, weeping, singing. He climbs the tree,
thrusting the vegetation aside. The face grins down
at him. He climbs and reaches it. And then he
laughs. His laughter, relief from pent-up fear,
echoes among the wailing voices, mingles with the
singing that comes from the face in the mid-

branches. He tears the face down from the branches and, holding it, climbs down on to the glimmering deadwood-littered ground.

The face is a square box, with the face painted on one side. On the other side is printed, "Milady Toilet Soap." Banjo strings are stretched across the open end of the box. Wiltshire strums his fingers across the strings, then ties the strings of the Aeolian harp on to his belt, picks up gun and lantern, and moves on. As he moves, so, every now and then, a puff of wind plays on the hanging face.

He reaches deep undergrowth. Here he has to force his way through, plying his knife as he goes, slicing the cords of liana, slashing down the great weeds. And still the other harps sing all around him in the trees. He struggles through undergrowth into a clearing.

In the clearing stands a high, druidical pile of ancient stones. And beyond it, a path. The path is very narrow, but well-beaten. He follows it and then stops dead. In front of him is a wall, tumble-down, very old, big-bouldered. The wall faces him, and along the top of it is a line of figures. They are little less than man-size and lurch and bob in the wind. The hidden harps sing as, cautiously, he approaches them. They have hideous carved and painted faces and shudder and twitch as if pulled by strings. Their limbs work with the tugging of the wind. Their eyes and teeth are made of shell. Their straw hair and their tribal garments blow in his face.

Suddenly Wiltshire jerks back with a start. A night bird silently dives down past him and tears at the hair of one of the figures lurching and bobbing there. Then, as Wiltshire moves, the bird flies off with a sharp single shriek.

And Wiltshire knocks the figure off the wall, tears of their clothes and hair, breaks the backs of them, rends their doll limbs, grinds their teeth and eyes under his heels. He knocks down and destroys figure after figure, all in a rage with them and his own now-forgotten fear.

But the last figure on the wall, a fat and grinning woman with a tattooed face, he slings, intact, over his shoulder.

He goes on, the wind harping the face he carries at his waist, the idol over his shoulder dancing. And, as he goes along the narrow, hindered path, snapping and cracking plants and branches aside, other hideous faces confront him, faces of figures cunningly hidden, cunningly fixed in the branches, so that at a touch they lollop forward, drunken and askew, grinning and trying to fondle. These he tears down ferociously.

Idols hang gibbeted from trees, their long clothes blow across his face, blinding him, their sickening painted grins fly on to his mouth. He knifes them down, slits and kicks them into the bush. He goes on through the peopled bush. Now an arm with a taloned hand hangs from a bough, and he tears it down. Other dismembered limbs sway from tree forks. He cuts them down with a fierce loathing, and slits them along so that their padding of grass and rushes trails out of them.

On a tree are painted two great slit eyes. He hacks his way on through this butcher's shop of the bush, and then—

He vanishes into the ground. One moment he is hacking his way in fury, and the next he is gone. The glimmering deadwood floor has swallowed him up.

From the man-high trap, into which he has fallen, comes a terrible squeaking, wailing, and hissing, hundreds of little voices. Wiltshire struggles and scrabbles in the dug pit. By the light of his dropped lantern, he sees that he is treading on a pool of little faces. He snatches up a handful of the faces. They are painted on balloons, balloons which, as he treads on them, let out air with a succession of squeaks and whistling grunts.

Clutching gun, lantern, and his handful of balloons, the idol figure lurching over his shoulder, he scrambles out of the pit. Once on the ground again, he pockets the balloons and goes at a rush through the bush. Now he reaches a long mound of earth, like a cromlech. The mound is at the edge of the path, which winds across the top of a sharp decline. He kicks away the earth.

With a cry, a head bounces out of the earth. But this time he is not startled. Quickly he grabs the head by the hair and drags it out. It is the head of a released jack-in-a-box, though unchildishly large and ghastly. He kicks it to pieces. And he kicks away the rest of the earth to find a tarpaulin sheet stretched across boards.

He looks around him, then at the sharp decline below the path. Rapidly he climbs down the decline and comes to the mouth of a cave. The roof of the cave is the tarpaulined boarding.

He goes into the cave. Rounding a corner, he brings, all of a sudden, his rifle to his shoulder. Then, after a moment, he walks warily on. In front of him, hanging from the roof of the cave is a skeleton. It is the skeleton of a full-grown man, but its face is monstrous. The face shines brilliantly. The brilliance waxes and dwindles, waxes and dwindles. Occasionally smoke floats out of it. Wiltshire goes nearer to the skeleton.

Wiltshire, softly: "Luminous paint, Mr. Case." He brings his lantern nearer the skeleton. Then with a harsh intake of breath, he bends down, the light of the lantern playing on the swaying legs and feet of the skeleton. One of the feet is clubbed.

Wiltshire, to himself, in a whisper: "Club-foot! So this is where you vanished, Johnny Adams." He cuts the rope from which the skeleton hangs, and lays it gently down on the floor of the cave. He covers the lurid, luminous face with his handkerchief.

Wiltshire: "Lie still now."

Wiltshire is going on again. The voices in the trees are still wailing. His stride is longer, easier, his whole poise less wary. He reaches a part of the bush where branches knit and knot darkly and inextricably over the path, putting out the moon. And out of the darkness a woman walks toward him.

He stops, as though frozen. He cannot raise his gun. He cannot move. The woman walks swiftly toward him, and the little high-voiced bells begin to ring. Wiltshire cries out. The woman is nearly on top of him. And then she speaks in an urgent voice: "Put out the lantern. It is me, Uma. Put it out. Hush. He is come."

Wiltshire puts out the lantern and, sighing with relief, moves as though to catch hold of her, but her urgency stops him still.

Uma: "Case is come. He is near in the bush. I heard him."

Again he moves toward her.

Uma, whispering: "No. Do not move. He will hear you. Faavo saw Little Jack outside the house tongiht. He listened. He listened to you saying

120

you would go find Tiapolo. Faavo saw him run to Case. She saw Case come up the path with a big gun."

Wiltshire, whispering: "Come along."

He takes her hand. Very softly they pad along the dark path, stray moonlight sieving through the laced leaves overhead. A gust of wind draws a wailing note from the box-harp at his waist. The idol figure lurches on his shoulder. With a tiny, muted cry, Uma presses closer to him.

Then, without warning, the dark, cavernous, cathedral-like arch of trees comes to an end, and Wiltshire and Uma are in bright moonlight. There is a flash and the screech of a bullet.

Uma pitches forward with a cry. Wiltshire flings himself forward beside her on the ground. Cautiously he raises himself on his elbows and bends over her. She lies crumpled up on one side.

Wiltshire, in an agonized whisper: "Uma, darling."

She turns her head slowly and smiles up at him through tears of pain.

Wiltshire: "Where? Where?"

She touches herself, very slowly and gently, above her left breast. Then her eyes close though she is still smiling. Wiltshire's face is vicious. He smiles too, but like an animal full of hate. His teeth are bared as though in a smile, but his hard eyes are shining.

Wiltshire, gently: "I'll get him, Uma. Smile at me, Uma. That's right. Smile all the time at me. Smile."

His voice is soft and low, and full of a kind of weedling affection: the voice one uses to humor a child. And as he says the words, very cautiously he is crawling away from her toward the part of the bush from where the bullet came, to where Case is lurking.

Wiltshire: "Don't worry, Uma. I'll get him. Always smile at me, Uma. I love you."

And with a sudden spring, he flings himself at the sheltering protecting of the bush at the side of the path. But as he springs there is another flash and report and the scream of a bullet.

The bullet catches him in mid-spring, throws him sideways in the air. And his rifle, also, is flung in the air and falls near the lying-down, crumpled figure of Uma.

Wiltshire is face downwards on the earth. Gingerly he slides his hand down his leg. His hand stops. He slides it up to his eyes. It is soaked in blood.

Very slowly, he snake-bellies his way toward Uma and the rifle. Then he tenses into stillness. Some little distance away there is the crack of a foot on brushwood. Case's head appears, white in the moonlight, over a wild wall of tall ferns. He raises his Winchester, levels it, fires.

Wiltshire squirms aside and is still. There is a dead stillness and silence. Then Case comes out of the ferns, his gun smoking. And as he comes out, spry, soft-footed, he laughs.

He comes up to Wiltshire, Wiltshire twisted and inert on the ground. And, behind Wiltshire, Uma crumpled in her white clothes. He comes very close to Wiltshire. And Wiltshire, with one galvanic movement, plucks the feet from under him.

Case falls cruelly and awkwardly, his rifle jerked out of his hands. His body thuds on the ground, and Wiltshire is on top of him.

Wiltshire: "Go on laughing. Smile at me, Uma. Laugh at me, Case."

His knife is open in his hand. Case fastens his teeth in his forearm, but Wiltshire heeds nothing. He does not attempt to shake off the weasel-like hold of Case's teeth. Wiltshire stabs Case in the body.

Wiltshire: "For Johnny Adams." And he stabs him again. "For Uma!"

Case twitches and lies still. Wiltshire rolls off him. He props himself up and bends over Case. Case's eyes are shut. But he speaks in the ghost of his dry, precise, mocking voice, slowly: "I did what evil I could. I should have been a politician. There is more scope. Is Uma dead?"

Wiltshire does not answer, stares down at the

thin, bitterly twisted dying lips and the shut eyes.

Case: "I wanted to make a clean sweep of you all tonight. It was my birthday. I wanted to kill you and Uma and Little Jack and Daddy Randall. Old friends—all of you. I poisoned Daddy's drink before leaving. I hope he shares the bottle with Little Jack. I think he will. He was always a generous man. Did I tell you it was my birthday today? I keep forgetting. Do you know how old I am?"

The thin twisted lips stiffen and then sag. Silence and stillness. Wiltshire stares close at the dead face.

Wiltshire: "You're very old now."

And a sudden wind sets the harp voices wailing. Wiltshire turns, crawling away.

There is a noise of voices and of feet crushing the underwood. The missionary, followed by Maea, comes through the bush, leading a party of men.

℘

The missionary is leading the men down through the bush above Falesá toward the village. Below can be seen the night fires of Falesá. Beyond them, the sounding sea.

Uma is being carried on a litter of branches. Wiltshire is limping along, supporting himself against one of Maea's braves, and Maea himself is bearing sack-wise over his shoulder the dead body of Case.

The party comes out of the bush by Case's bungalow. The bearers carry Uma on toward the village. Maea, followed limpingly by Wiltshire and his supporting native, walks up the veranda steps, Case over his shoulder. He flings the door open.

In the trading room, where a lit lamp hangs from the roof, Little Jack and Captain Randall sit at the table, their heads sunken. On the table in front of them is a half empty bottle and two glasses. Also on the table, directly before them, are their two fiddles, the bows by the side. At the top of the table there is one unoccupied chair. And on the table in front of that chair lies Case's concertina.

Maea comes into the room, followed by Wiltshire and his attendant. Maea slumps Case down into the unoccupied chair directly facing the concertina. The three dead men sit before their instruments. Wiltshire stands at the door.

Wiltshire, slowly: "You wouldn't think they were dead. You'd think they were going to play."

He stares at the three dead men and the fiddles and the concertina.

The missionary, Maea, Wiltshire, and his attendant walk toward Wiltshire's bungalow where Uma is lying in bed in the living room. The missionary bandages her shoulder. She is smiling. Wiltshire bends down over her.

The stars of the night fires are burning in the village. As though from the inside of Case's bungalow, comes the gay music of fiddles and concertina.

And beyond the bungalow, the gay music continues to the beach of Falesá.